U0068170

小說的密碼

人性—與—關懷

涂成吉—————— 編著

自 序

　　全世界七十億人口中，最不妥協的一件事，就是我們絕不見一雙相同指紋，這象徵著每一個人都是獨特的，也正因人性的深不可測，如同指尖紋路，千變萬化，有人性始有文學，有人性始有小說，小說正是發掘此一人心深邃無底多樣的生命故事。

　　本書最大目的，就是希望學子在最少的閱讀挫折下，對英文小說文學，有最快的入門，編製上，書中的作者短評與作品分析，固然有助文選的親近，但最大的挑戰還是如何讓學生不因艱澀與冗長的英文，而降低閱讀原文的熱度與動力，否則一切也是惘然。因此，筆者在不失原味下，精簡原著篇幅，並將英文生字的解說，不擺設在他頁，而是直接安插其後，保持閱讀流暢，不致讓欣賞的感覺中斷。最後，在原作的應用上，配以活潑的朗讀、表演或發揮想像的作業延伸，完就一本兼具程度又好讀、悅讀的英美小說文學精選。

　　除首篇《導論》外，本書過濾與精選了分具浪漫、寫實、自然與現代主義，風格明確、主題突出的十九篇英文經典短篇小說。不論作者或作品，大皆耳熟能詳，極富個人寫作特徵之代表。大致歸納如下：

所謂「人心惟危」，「求生」成了小說中，一個極佳發掘人性的題材，史蒂芬‧克蘭的《海上扁舟》與傑克‧倫敦《生火》分別在大海及北國冰天雪地中，寫下了兩種截然不同氛圍的美國自然主義小說佳作。

　　如果你喜歡享受surprise或跌碎眼鏡的快感，愛倫‧坡《弗德馬先生案的真相》黑色劇，歐亨利《最後一片葉子》的急轉彎，畢爾斯《梟河橋記事》的驚愕，法蘭克史塔頓《美女還是老虎？》的兩難，應該是不會使你失望的選擇。馬克吐溫《好小孩的故事》，一貫呈現他小說鄉土、直接的口語幽默，妙趣橫生，讀著讀著，總讓人不斷腦海浮現《湯姆歷險記》中，那位靈活、頑皮，一身是膽的西部小孩，才是馬克吐溫渴望的美國人格典型。

　　人生哲理，梅爾維爾《提琴手》，王爾德《自私的巨人》，則分別以嚴肅與童話兩種方式表達生命中捨得、分享，平淡的意境。

　　小說也是精準抓住一個社會當時經濟、政治及歷史意義的語言密碼。海明威《白象似的群山》與史考特‧費茲傑羅《一個酗酒案例》，將美國二〇年代所謂「失落的一代」，性、女人、酒的空虛頹廢，一語道盡。

　　凱特‧蕭邦《一小時的故事》與威廉福克納《給愛蜜麗的玫瑰》，前者以出乎意表的結局諷刺，後者卻充滿黑色、壓抑的恐怖謀殺，表達對美國女性主義的悲觀。

　　二十紀後，現代小說傾向個人內心更潛深處探索的「意識流」派，霍桑《年輕的布朗大爺》與二十世紀的喬伊斯《伊芙琳》和伍爾芙《一間鬼屋》，古今相比，讓小說又有不同境界的閱讀感受。

狄更斯《兒童的故事》與薛吾德安德森《林中之死》分別是十九、二十世紀，抗議資本文明生活下，對個人生活扭曲，前者藉一旅人的淡定與後者由一婦人的沉重，分釋了現代生死的奧秘。

當然上述筆者的整理，只是一個極大簡略的分類，因為每篇小說裏，都有相當不同複雜的元素、手法與象徵的可議。然筆者個人倒是在這十九篇文章中，發現一些共同或者心得：

一、創作幾乎不外是個人生活經驗呈現，所以每個人都可以是小說家。

二、生死問題常涉大部文章主軸。

三、也許是時代巧合，這些小說家大部晚景淒涼，不得善終，極端例如伍爾芙，不知這是天份作家之宿命或curse？

作者民國一〇二年七月於內湖

Contents

導論
——有人性始有文學，有人性始有小說

一、小說與人性

　　大底言，西方現代小說的巨浪，洶湧於十九世紀中的「浪漫主義」思潮。當知識份子開始質疑「啟蒙時代」所推崇理性、秩序與和諧的這些想法，轉而強調個人心靈、獨特性與想像力的特點時，浪漫主義才正式宣告人類始祖亞當、夏娃因對上帝「說謊」，而生西方「原罪性惡」的結束。

　　也就是當人類由「神本」的迷信，邁進「人本」自信，卻是浪漫主義使人性更進一步自理性而至感性的解放，從此，不但人情的正面：善、智慧與良知，取得認同；同時對人性的負面：自私、妒嫉與憎恨，也能包容探索，這是西方大不同中國儒家人性本善，一昧去惡存善的固執，卻讓小說的內容更客觀接近人性寬廣與複雜的真實。蓋有人性始有文學，有人性始有小說，正因人性之深不可測，各人性格之千變萬化，小說正是發掘此一人心無底深邃多樣之生命故事。

二、天堂、審判、重生：神本至人本之路

　　雖說人性是小說的中心內涵，但人性的自由解脫，卻是一段長遠逐步的歷程，也因人性之神秘深邃，這段摸索路途亦將歷久不休。至少就目前的歷程，小說與「人性」歷史蛻變，可略帶分成以下原罪、理性與感性三階段：

　　（1）、宗教迷信：神本（原罪信仰）

　　（2）、哲學理性：人本（啟蒙理性至文藝復興，自然神論）

　　（3）、資本主義社會：個人存在價值與自我的剖析。

（一）、天堂——人性枷鎖期：性惡、神本、壓抑。

　　就人類歷史言，宗教常是第一個對人性解釋的權威，也是影響最深遠的心靈桎梏。以基督教「原罪論」來看，西方歷一千四百年，才得到解脫，然餘威猶巨。那探索「人之初」，西方造物主——耶和華的理想人性設計或說祂是要怎樣的人類呢？從上古文學的兩大巨著之一，【聖經】首篇《創世紀》內容來看，自〈神造亞當與夏娃〉，夏娃背叛上帝吃了「知識之果」（蘋果背了幾千年的黑鍋），逐出伊甸園，以至〈諾亞方舟〉，上帝見人性頑劣之無可救贖，以大洪水全面毀滅人類止。我們大略可清楚理出，神原本是不望人有想法，一旦人有慾望，人性之惡，罄竹難書，無奈亞當、夏娃的背叛，最終只好妥協，望有如亞伯拉罕、約伯者，以神為本，信仰為念：

　　（1）、亞當與夏娃：說謊、羞恥。

（2）、該隱與亞伯：憤怒、妒嫉、謀殺。

（3）、巴別塔：自大、傲慢。

（4）、諾亞方舟：神毀滅人類。

（5）、亞伯拉罕：信心之父。

（6）、約伯的故事。

（二）、審判——人性解放期：人本、反教、理性

至西元約十五世紀，不知是否亞當與夏娃在伊甸園吃的知識之果，開始發酵，十七、十八世紀，人類進入啟蒙運動，人神關係改變，理性開始凌駕信仰：

（1）、自由神論：宇宙不過是井然有序的時鐘，即是無所不能的神，也不能隨心所欲，反復無常。

（2）、唯理性主義：

　　・人可以由「經驗」而理性（唯物）。

　　・我思故我在（唯心）。

　　・除了懷疑，一切皆可懷疑。

　　・無知是罪（sin）。

　　・大航海時代：The World is not Flat.

（三）重生——文藝復興：那到底真正人性何在？

西方重新對希臘羅馬文學發生興趣，由【伊里雅德】、【奧狄賽】而出之【希臘神話】中，他們看到希臘眾神性格動人、真實、有趣，與威權的耶和華相比，希臘眾神與人有一樣的喜怒哀樂情緒。人性與神格何異？

（1）、普羅米修斯：與【聖經】《創世紀》相較，普羅米修斯等於是【希臘神話】中，創造人類的上帝，普羅米修斯一樣按神的形象，用泥土塑造了人類，過程極盡相似，但兩帝個性卻完全是倒過來寫的，普羅米修斯相較【聖經】中上帝對待人類嚴厲態度，普羅米修斯卻是深愛人類，他盜神火予人間，還教人類對神說謊，氣得宙斯先派潘朵拉——等於【聖經】中的夏娃，來滅絕人類不成，再以大洪水毀滅，普羅米修斯都盡力保護人類的生存。

（2）、宙斯：【希臘神話】中的萬神之神，不是普羅米修斯，而是宙斯，宙斯生性風流，為得與人間美女一夜情，是不擇手段，雖老犯全天下男人都會犯的錯，卻又是PTT之祖，但有時又有男人負責到底的勇氣。

（3）、希拉：宙斯妻子，雖貴為天后，整天忙著抓小三，一旦醋罈子打翻，發起狠來，對情敵是不留活口，但與宙斯私生之海克力士的一段經過，又是母性十足。除宙斯不倫戀外，【希臘神話】中對愛情的著墨最多，談起戀愛，眾神一如人生自是有情癡的動人。各式各樣的愛憎，茲舉數例：

（1）、特洛依戰爭：是一個女人（Helen）的戰火？還是三個女人的妒火？

（2）、納西瑟思的自戀。

（3）、維納斯的劈腿戰神。

（4）、阿波羅與達芙妮。

（5）、歌神奧菲斯。

（6）、潘恩與西林克斯。

（7）、月神戴安娜與安迪米翁。

文藝復興時代，人性多樣化（variety）的複雜表現，也影響到地方文學的啟發，英國莎士比亞在他著名悲劇中，也暗示：有情人不終成眷屬——《羅蜜歐與茱麗葉》，好人不一定勝利——《李爾王》、《哈姆雷特》，正直不一定戰勝妒嫉——《喜塞羅》、權力慾望勝過忠誠——《馬克白》。西班牙塞萬提的《唐吉訶德》——人為理想也要有傻勁。

藝術此刻也起了人性的革命，象徵基督教威權鬆動之波提切利〈維納斯的誕生〉，達文西〈耶穌最後的晚餐〉，最富啟發性代表則屬米開蘭基羅作品中的〈創世紀〉、〈逐出伊甸園〉、〈最後的審判〉，試想當他以希臘文藝復興的人文反教主義者，詮釋基督教人類之創造與毀滅，他腦海的聖經人物造型，該是以誰為靈感呢？我們從米開蘭基羅以充滿彈性線條與完美身軀的人體裸露，展現人間七情六慾，他根本是以希臘眾神的形體作上帝與亞當模樣的結合，呈現最完美的「反動」密碼，在〈聖殤〉中，耶穌與瑪麗亞聖母更宛若喪失戀人的悲慟。

三、浪漫主義與現代主義：感性重於理性。

十九世紀中葉以後，工業革命、法國大革命、進化論、與資本主義的人類連環歷史事件的發生，產生強大民族國家、中產階級與個人財富。相對理性主義反使世界失去生機，有如死灰，何況，人生有常？抑無常？理性思考也無法解答萬一，人此時卻是益發的自信只要跟著感覺走，結果難脫美好，代表人物盧梭在《懺悔錄》寫下「我敢說我這個人就是和別人不一樣。就算我不比別人好，起碼我跟別人不一樣。」，「浪漫主義」應時而生，個人感性開始重於理性，感覺代替思考，小說也得到最多的想像與空間。然而，過度的資本功利，複雜的社會、政經問題，這些同樣的社會元素，也興起「寫實主義」與「自然主義」，轉而筆觸人心客觀真實題材，關注社會周遭變化，幻想之地與遙不可及都在寫作排除之列和「浪漫主義」主觀、心靈與小我的思考有清楚的對比。

二十紀後，拜科技文明日新月異之賜，當人類有更多人定勝天的例子時，尤當人類完成登陸月球的天梯，彷彿又回到〈巴別塔〉的狂放，照理，人類可更「造反」有理，矛盾是：我們慶幸人類反思的能力克制了這股傲慢與自大，反憂慮的是：當宗教「信我得永生」的簡明概念漸褪，個人的永生為何？人類的幸福能一直下去嗎？有人開始對存在價值產生懷疑，這以「自我」為創作基礎，發掘人的內心活動，出現了頹廢派、荒誕派、象徵主義、虛無主義、意識流等小說，使小說的本質發生了變異，此乃「現代主義」崛起。

四、結論

現代小說除是文學與語言的結合，直接探訪人性的真實外，更望讀者於欣賞中，也能看到小說背後的社會意義，增長思考批判的能力，培養人文關懷的精神。畢竟小說創意的來源，莫過你必需保持對人的興趣，願意想像人內心的動靜，瞭解真人的本質。這也是筆者多少憂慮，相對日益強大的網路世界，多少剝奪了人的相處與想像，畢竟，人與人還是必須真實的接觸，有眼神、音調的交會，才有人性的真情感受；這也是每當看到越來越多年輕朋友低頭專注在智慧手機、臉書、線上遊戲的虛擬天地中，那般滿足、沉醉時，我總感覺亞當、夏娃彷彿又重返上帝的伊甸園了！

五、閱讀文選

The Genesis
~ Bible

　　Long ago, before the world began, there was darkness everywhere. So God decided to make light to shine into the darkness. He called the light "day" and the darkness he called "night." This was the first day.

　　Then God *parted*（分開）the sky and seas. This was the second day. From the seas dry land *appear*（出現）. On this *empty*（空曠）and *lifeless*（沒有生命的）land, God created beautiful, green trees and *plants*（植物）with colorful flowers and *luscious*（美味的）fruit. He filled the fruit with *seeds*（種子）so that more plants and trees could grow. This was the third day.

　　God was pleased with his world, so He went on to make two lights, called the sun and the moon, in the sky. These were to separate（分隔）day from night and act as *signs*（記號）mark the seasons, days, and years. God made the moon and stars to give out a gentler light at night. This was the fourth day.

Now I shall fill my world with living *creatures*（生物）, thought God. He made the birds to fly in the sky, fish to swim in the seas, and all kinds of animals, both great and small, to *roam*（倘佯）on the land. He told the creatures to have young and *multiply*（繁衍）so that they would *spread over*（散播）all the earth. This was the fifth day.

God was happy with everything that he had made, so He decided to make people to enjoy his creation and take care of it. On the sixth day, first God created a man named Adam. He put Adam among the beautiful trees and plants of the *garden of Eden*（伊甸園）. Then, to keep Adam *company*（陪伴）, God made a woman named Eve. Adam and Eve lived happily in the garden of *Eden* and God *provided*（提供）everything they needed. In the middle of the garden were two special trees. One was called *the tree of life*（永生之樹）. The other was called the tree of the Knowledge of Good and Evil. God told Adam, "You may eat from any tree in the garden, but you must not eat from *the Tree of the Knowledge of Good and Evil*（善惡的知識之樹）, for if you do you will surely die."

God was pleased with the world He had done. So, He wanted all the people to rest in order to *worship*（崇拜）Him on the seventh day.

The enemy of God, the *devil*（魔鬼）, decided to make Adam and Eve *disobey*（違背）God's command. He used a *crafty*（狡滑）snake to *persuade*（說服）Eve to eat from the *forbidden*（禁止的）tree. The snake told her that if she did this she would become as *wise*（智慧）as God.

So Eve ate from the tree and *tempted*（引誘）Adam to eat, too. As soon as they had disobey God and eaten, Adam and Eve knew right from wrong, and they were *ashamed*（羞恥）. God was very angry. He *cursed*（詛咒）the snake and *banished*（驅逐）Adam and Eve from the garden of Eden. Because they could no longer reach the Tree of Life, Adam and Eve could not eat its fruit live for ever. "from now on Adam will have to work hard for what you need to live and Eve will *suffer from*（受苦）the pain to *bear a child*（生小孩）." said God.

Adam and Eve had chosen to disobey God. Now they had to make their own way in the world.

六、作品延伸與作業

希臘神話中眾神人物其實也是某些領導流行時尚（fashion）的品牌名稱，妳知道是哪些知名的精品？除此之外，還有哪些領域，也以希臘神話人物命名？

2 詹姆士・古柏《日蝕》
——美國本土文學拓荒者

小說特徵

美國本土自然風光、拓荒者
與印地安人戰爭的邊疆故事

詹姆士・古柏
(James F. Cooper, 1789–1851)

The affairs of life embrace a multitude of interests, and he who reasons in any one of them, is a visionary.

-James F. Cooper

生活的事務包含著多重趣味，凡事以理性看待，則成虛幻。

——詹姆士・古柏

一、作者短評

　　詹姆士・古柏，1789年生於紐澤西，家世富裕，父親是大地主、國會議員，一歲，詹姆士移居紐約古柏鎮，這由他父親之名，所建城鎮。古柏十三歲即至耶魯大學就讀，卻因為頻頻惡作劇，像是炸掉同學的房門，讓驢子跳到老師背上，而被踢出校門，可見古柏年少放蕩不羈的個性。離開學校後，古柏上了商船，作了水手；十八歲，加入美國海軍。

　　古柏成名之作《皮襪的故事》（The Leatherstocking Tales），是由《拓荒者》（The Pioneers, 1823）、《最後的摩希根人》（The Last of the Mohicans, 1826）、《大草原》（The Prairie, 1827）、《開路人》（The Pathfinder, 1840）、《殺鹿人》（The Deerslayer,1841）五部作品的合成，系列描寫美國殖民地時期，英、法軍隊在北美洲的殖民戰爭；與獨立拓荒時代，西部移民與印地安族群的戰爭故事。 其中，最耳熟能詳代表之作──《最後的摩希根人》（The Last of the Mohicans），好萊塢也改拍成，由丹尼爾戴路易斯（Daniel Day Lewis）主演之電影《大地英豪》。敘述一位由印地安人撫養長大的白人，轉而對抗來自英、法統治殖民的殺戮，隱喻新大陸的善與舊世界（歐洲）的惡，文中除表達美國本土印地安人對自然的尊重與共生的和諧，譬如印地安人對所獵殺動物，會表達惺惺相惜之意，但也暗表白人在新大陸移民擴張中對印地安人的迫害，以致族群滅絕的悲慘遭遇。

古柏，1826年，因發展寫作事業，而移居歐洲，直到1833年，才返鄉定居古柏鎮的Otsego Hall，期間一度改採政治內容的寫作，卻不受讀者青睞，才重拾拓荒者與印地安人戰爭的邊疆故事，而完成後續之《開路人》與《殺鹿人》。1851年，古柏在家鄉過世。

二、作品分析

　　美國自1776年獨立建國起，至十九世紀中，不過百年，國力與財富就有獨步全球氣勢；惟文學上，美國人民仍醉心英國文學書刊與小說，惟英國作家所見是瞻，這般文學依賴現象，無怪1802年，英國文學批評家希尼・史密斯（Sydney Smith）：「在本世紀，誰讀過一本美國人寫的書？誰看過美國人寫的歌劇？誰曾觀賞過美國人所作一幅畫或一件雕刻？」，這一俐落話語雖失之尖酸，卻也深刻道白當時美國文學成就上的貧乏自卑。

　　在感慨美國雖然政治獨立，卻仍然是英國文學附庸的事實，詹姆士・古柏可謂是第一位能吸引轉移國內讀者，轉注美國文學的拓荒之士。而使古柏創作，有別歐洲舊大陸者，正是他引用新大陸之壯闊山川、原始林木及原住民印地安人的本土素材，作為他創作內容和靈感。

　　古柏的創作大部來自他個人的生活精經驗。古柏自幼成長紐約州中部，幼年即見識西部拓展甘苦，親睹西部拓荒中，移民與印地安人及大自然博鬥、共生過程，而生迷戀之情，轉而以西部拓荒者與印地安人生活為小說題材，探討個人與自然關係，雕塑美國人獨立、自由、理想及道德形象，也因為古柏的成功，才激勵1830年代之後，一群來自美國東北部新英格蘭地區（New England）的文學人士如愛默生（R. W. Emerson）、霍桑（Nathaniel Hawthorne）、惠特曼（Walt Whiteman）等許多卓越的文學家和思想家，發起國家文學解放運動，造就美國本土民族文學理論——「超越主義」[1]（Transcendentalism）的誕生，使美國文學從模仿英國及歐洲大陸的風格中，脫穎開創了美國文藝復興，幫助美國人完成了文學立國之夢。

　　本文所選古柏短篇小說《日蝕》，其實正是古柏回憶1806年6月16日，發生在他北美故鄉Otsego的日蝕奇景，文中描述了家鄉的青山、湖泊、樹林、田野、峭壁與洞穴，一切有如「老友臉龐般親切」。而村民在期待日蝕的時光中，大為平淡的生活增添一絲興奮，古柏敘述了許多日蝕的珍奇自然現象如露水不斷的降下，萬鳥不啼，蝙蝠盤旋，天象上，星星更見閃爍，閃電、濃雲的出現，當月亮將日光搶奪，每天村鎮午時的熱浪瞬間消去，氣溫驟降，當光明重返山谷，內心的感動與振奮，又讓親身體會者有股莫名的激動，古柏將之比擬「基督的回聲，教導人類學習謙卑的一課」，讓古柏深刻體會照造物者之神奇與最深的敬畏。

---

[1]　超越主義（Transcendentalism）是十九世紀，美國本土文人響應浪漫文學運動下而生之國家民族文學運動，發起人愛默生為超越文學定義：「超越主義者主張心靈主義聯想，相信奇蹟、啟發與極度喜悅。我們對先人所言，常不假思索的採信，怯於自我實現。超越主義者是決不流於世俗，只作自己。」

三、閱讀文選

The Eclipse

James F. Cooper

The *eclipse of the sun*（日蝕）*occurred*（發生）in the summer of 1806, on Monday, the 16th of June. I was then on a visit to my parents, at the home of my family, among the Highlands of Otsego, in that part of the country where the eclipse was *most impressive*（最印象深刻之地）.

Throughout（整個）the belt of country to be darkened by the eclipse, the whole *population*（人口）were in a *state of*（一個…狀態）*anxious expectation*（渴望的期待）for weeks before the event. *On the eve of*（前夕）the 16th of June, our *family circle*（家族）could think or talk of little else. We were all *exulting*（瘋狂興奮）in the feeling that a *grand and extraordinary spectacle*（壯麗、不凡的景象）awaited us—a spectacle which millions then living could never *behold*（看得到）. There may have been *a tinge of*（一絲…的）selfishness in the feeling that we were *favored*（受寵幸）beyond others.

And the first movement in the morning was to the open window—again to examine the sky. As yet there was no change *perceptible*（感受得到）in the sunlight falling upon lake and mountain; *bright and glowing*（光華如火）as on other days of

June. Gradually a fifth, and even a fourth, of the *sun's disc*（太陽圓碟）, became *obscured*（遮蔽）. The noon—day heat, however, began to lessen, and something of the coolness of early morning returned to the valley.

A great change had taken place. The trees on the distant *heights*（高地）had lost their *verdure*（翠綠）and their *airy character*（清新的特質）. The lake wore a *lurid aspect*（如火紅似的外觀）, very unusual. All living *creatures*（生物）seemed thrown into a state of *agitation*（騷動）. The birds were *fluttering to and fro*（慌張地前後來去）, in great excitement; they seemed to *wonder if*（驚奇；懷疑）this was the *approach*（接近）of evening, and were undecided in their movements. Even the dogs—honest *creatures*（生物）—became uneasy, and drew closer to their masters.

As the light failed more and more with every passing second, the children came *flocking about*（聚集在）their mothers in terror. The women themselves were looking about uneasily for their husbands. The men were very generally silent and grave. The birds had been *fluttering about*（翅膀急促地拍打）in great agitation, seemed now *convinced*（確信）that night was at hand. Swallows were seen dropping into the *chimneys*（煙囪）, the *martins*（燕子的一種）returned to their little boxes, the *pigeons*（鴿子）flew home to their dove—cots, and we saw *the fowls going to roost*（家禽；雞回巢）.

The *dew*（露水）was falling *perceptibly*（相當地）, and the coolness was so great that the *thermometer*（溫度計）must have fallen many degrees from the great heat of the morning. The lake, the hills, and the buildings of the little town were *swallowed up in*（吞噬於）the darkness. The song of the summer birds, so full in June, had *entirely ceased*（完全地停止）for the last half hour. A bat came *flitting about*（急速飛掠）our heads.

At twelve minutes past eleven, the *gloom*（幽暗）of night was upon us. Many stars were now *visible*（可以看見）, though not in *sufficient number*（數量足以）to lessen the darkness. The peaceful rainbow, the heavy clouds of a great storm, the *vivid flash of electricity*（鮮明的電光閃爍）, the falling *meteor*（隕石）, *fickle*（多變如）as the play of fancy（奇幻）.

The *sensation*（感人轟動的大事）created by this *majestic*（壯麗的）spectacle had been one of *humiliation and awe*（屈辱與敬畏）. It seemed as if the great Father of the Universe had *veiled*（遮掩）his face in *wrath*（憤怒）. I shall only say that I have beheld spectacle which so *plainly manifested*（明白地證明）the majesty of the *Creator*（造物主；上帝）, so *forcibly*（強勢地）taught the lesson of *humility*（謙卑）to man as a total eclipse of the sun.

四、作品延伸與作業

如以英文短篇小說的文創方式，作吸引臺灣特色之國際行銷，妳有無動人的本土景觀或自然現象的構想創意？妳可以用306個鄉鎮之風光為例。

3 霍桑《年輕的布朗大爺》
——善與惡的人性交叉

小說特徵

人本、反清教、善與惡之對立

納撒尼爾 · 霍桑
(Nathaniel Hawthorne , 1804-1864)

There is evil in every human heart, which may remain latent, perhaps, through the whole life; but circumstances may rouse it to activity.

-Nathaniel Hawthorne

每一個人的內心都有邪惡，也許會潛伏一生，但也有被喚醒活動的時候。

——納撒尼爾· 霍桑

一、作者短評

　　納撒尼爾・霍桑（Nathaniel Hawthorne），1804年，出生於美國麻塞諸塞州賽倫（Salem），全鎮充滿濃厚之清教氣息，霍桑全家皆為清教徒[2]（Puritans），清教主義的幽暗背景，於人性和心靈的壓制和摧殘，對霍桑的思想及創作產生了極大的影響，被譽為美國19世紀最具影響的浪漫主義小說家。

　　清教徒重視道德與努力工作，一切以教義為尊，壓制人心，這也是何以清教思想總予美國人一股愛、憎交雜的情緒，愛的是它堅毅執著的宗教情懷，孕育出代表美國人民獨特的理想性格；憎的也是他一絲不苟，不容挑戰的價值權威，將人性束縛在他如鋼鐵般的教義紀律之中。清教徒排斥感情，崇尚禁慾簡樸，以教義為生活指導，不但迫害異己，採取的是政教合一的神道政權形式，霍桑家族先後在迫害桂格（Quaker）教派的「獵巫案」（witch hunting）中扮演過不光彩的角色，家族的這一段歷史使霍桑成人後的在心理，始終懷有愧罪感。

　　1842年，霍桑移居康考特（Concord），結識了美國本土版的浪漫主義——「超越主義」（Transcendentalism）作家如：愛默生、梅爾維爾、梭羅等人，「超越主義」作家由於對人性有

---

[2] 英國國王亨利八世，一五三四年，也加入宗教革命運動，自立英國國教（Church of England），但亨利八世動機只是因個人婚姻問題不得羅馬教皇祝福而反舊教，故目的達成後，對改革舊教一事自敷衍了事，而堅持去除舊教於國教者則被以清教徒稱之。

更高信心，巧的是該地也正是清教大本營，這使清教思想，勢所難免地與超越文學衝突。文學創作上，超越主義也的確針對清教思想於個人自由與在現實生活中的壓抑人性，莫不口誅筆伐，相信人格一如神格，可止於至善。

霍桑抨擊清教食古不化和教會虛偽，慣用象徵手法，揭示人物內心衝突和心理描寫，作品往往帶有濃厚的宗教氣氛和神祕色彩，霍桑和愛倫‧坡一樣喜好運用一些超自然的元素，並且同樣具有美學而不是宗教的基礎，但不同愛倫‧坡小說上強調「恐怖娛樂」的效果，霍桑總是更關注倫理和哲學方面的思考和探索，這就使他的作品總是蘊含着令人回味不盡的深邃哲理，故文學史家常把他列為浪漫主義作家，長篇小說《紅字》公認是霍桑最成功之作，姐妹之作的短篇小說《年輕的布朗大爺》探索個人內心善惡作之轉變，文筆之洗鍊，是虛是實的寫作，媲美二十世紀初期的「意識流」與「魔幻寫實」小說的先驅之作，霍桑在美國文學史上的地位也更為確定。

南北戰爭爆發後，霍桑的身體每況愈下，1864年5月19日在美國新罕布夏州樸次茅斯去世。他的墓碑只簡單地由一塊普通的石頭做成，上面僅刻着他的姓氏：霍桑。

二、作品分析

美國基礎上是以清教價值立國。一六二〇年，這批來自英國的清教徒，因見清除英國國教中天主教殘餘制度無望，乃搭乘「五月花號」（Mayflower），移民北美麻塞諸塞，希望建立一純粹基督徒社會的「新耶路撒冷」，從此被奉為美國人最早祖先。

由於霍桑出身清教家庭，清教傳統對他影響很深，這種思想滲透到他的作品中，使他一方面擺脫不掉「原罪」、「贖罪」、「內省」和「命定」之類的清教教義；但又從家族的負罪感出發，反過來對清教的專制統治痛心疾首。因此，一方面他反抗這個傳統，抨擊清教狹隘、虛偽的教條；另一方面他又受這個傳統的束縛，以清教的善惡觀念來認識社會和整個世界，這也是他大部作品中滲透着「人本」和「原罪」的對立觀。

霍桑的短篇小說《年輕的布朗大爺》正是揭露清教的虛偽，人人皆有的隱祕罪惡，表達了人性是善與惡交纏的矛盾觀點，特別是其中有許多象徵的意涵，點出象徵技巧在文學作品的運用及重要性，被視為霍桑最佳典型的短篇小說。

故事敘及青年牧師布朗在某日落時分，也沒說明理由，告別取名「信心」（Faith）的妻子，到黑暗的森林中，途中遇見一帶著「蛇杖」（snake staff）象徵撒旦的旅人，誘惑他參與一場魔鬼的聚會，所經歷一夜個人內心善與惡的交戰。文中的布朗基本就是霍桑本人的心境寫照，魔鬼撒旦在誘惑布朗時，其中，談到如何協助他祖父在「獵巫」運動中，虐殺桂格教派女子及燒殺印地安人，反映霍桑最引以為疚的個人家族歷史，布朗起先靠著「上天與妻子信心」的支持下，抵抗邪惡對善的引誘。

但當布朗發現全村的要人，包括他幼時讀經班老師，視同「精神與道德的導師」Goody Closse太太也赴會，最終，連妻子

「信心」竟也參與了魔鬼信徒的聚會，導致他信仰的崩潰，可見「如今世界已無善，只剩邪惡」：

> *"My Faith is gone!" cried he, after one stupefied moment. "There is no good on earth; and sin is but a name. Come, devil; for to thee is this world given."*

　　布朗走入黑暗難測森林之旅的象徵意義，代表著其內心趨向罪惡的本質，雖然他在緊要關頭抗拒了撒旦的誘惑，但在第二天回到村莊後，這像夢境一般的魔鬼聚會的遭遇，使布朗心靈卻再也沒有恢復平靜，他迴避妻子「信心」，且不時想起那夜在森林中的魔鬼頌歌，最後抑鬱而終。至於小說看完後的兩大疑問：這是一場夢？妻子「信心」最後是否抵抗了魔鬼的誘惑？反都不具太大意義。

Young Goodman Brown

Nathaniel Hawthorne

Young Goodman Brown came into the street at Salem village at sunset; but put his head back to exchange a *parting kiss*（吻別） with his young wife. And Faith, *as the wife was aptly*（巧妙地） named, "Dearest heart," whispered she, softly and sadly, when her *lips*（雙唇） were close to his ear, "please put off your *journey*（旅程） until sunrise and sleep in your own bed tonight. Pray stay with me this night, dear husband, of all nights in the year."

"My love and my Faith," replied young Goodman Brown, "of all nights in the year, this one night must I stay away from you. My *journey*（旅程） must need be done between now and sunrise. "

So they *parted*（分手） and the young man *pursued his way*（趕路）；he looked back and saw the head of Faith still *peeping after*（偷看著） him with a *melancholy air*（憂鬱的神色）.

With this excellent *resolve*（決心） for the future, Goodman Brown had taken a *dreary*（淒涼；陰暗） road, darkened by all the gloomiest trees of the forest. It was all as lonely as could be; and strange in such a *solitude*（孤獨）.

His head being turned back, he passed a *crook*（彎曲） of the road, and, looking forward again, *beheld*（看到） a man in *decent attire*

（端莊的衣著）, seated at the foot of an old tree. He arose at Goodman Brown's approach and walked onward *side by side*（並肩）with him.

"You are late, Goodman Brown," said he.

"Faith kept me back a while," replied the young man, with a *tremor*（顫抖）in his voice, caused by the sudden appearance of his *companion*（伴隨）.

As nearly as could be *discerned*（目光所見）, the traveler was about fifty years old, and *bearing a considerable resemblance*（極端相似）to him. But the only thing about him that could be *fixed upon*（專注的）was his staff（手仗）*in the shape*（以…形狀）of a great black snake, *twisting and wriggling*（蠕動爬行）itself like a living *serpent*（毒蛇）.

"Come, Goodman Brown. Take my staff, if you are so soon *weary.*（疲憊）" cried his fellow-traveler. "Well, Goodman Brown! I have *been as well acquainted with*（熟識）your family as a Puritan. I helped your grandfather when he *lashed*（痛鞭；暗指殘害）the *Quaker*（貴格教派）woman so smartly through the streets of Salem; and it was I that brought your father a *pitch-pine*（松脂油）, *kindled*（點燃）at my own *hearth*（火爐）, to set fire to an Indian village. They were my good friends, both; and many a pleasant walk have we had along this path, and returned merrily after midnight. I would be friends with you *for their sake*（看在他們的份上）."

"I *marvel*（訝異）they never spoke of these matters. We are a people of prayer, and good works, and *abide*（容忍）no such *wickedness*（邪惡）," replied Goodman Brown.

"Ha! ha! ha!" shouted he again and again; then *composing*（回復鎮靜）himself, "Well, go on, Goodman Brown, go on; but, please, don't kill me with laughing."

As he spoke he *pointed*（指向）his staff at a female figure on the path, in whom Goodman Brown *recognized*（認出）a very *pious and exemplary dame*（虔誠模範的女士）—Goody Closse, who had taught him his *catechism*（教義問答）in youth, and was still his *moral and spiritual adviser*（道德與精神的導師）, jointly with the *minister*（牧師）and Deacon Gookin.

Young Goodman Brown looked up to the sky, doubting whether there really was a heaven above him.

"With heaven above and Faith below, I will yet stand firm against the devil!" cried Goodman Brown.

The next moment, so *indistinct*（不清楚）were the sounds, there was one voice of a young woman. "It is Faith!" shouted Goodman Brown, in a voice of *agony and desperation*（痛苦與絕望）; and the *echoes*（回音）of the forest *mocked*（嘲弄）him, crying, "Faith! Faith!" as if seeking her all through the *wilderness*（荒野）.

The cry of *grief, rage, and terror*（悲傷、憤怒與恐懼）was yet *piercing the night*（穿透夜空）. "My Faith is gone!" cried he. "There is no good on earth; and sin is but a name. Come, devil; for to you is this world given."

Maddened with despair, Goodman Brown went at such a *rate*（速度）that he seemed to fly along the forest path , until he saw a red light before him, he paused, and heard a *hymn*（聖歌）. He knew the tune; it was a familiar one in the *choir*（唱詩班）of the village meeting—house.

At an open space, *hemmed in*（圍繞於）the dark wall of the forest, arose a rock, *bearing resemblance to a pulpit*（像是一祭壇）, and *surrounded by*（被..圍繞）four *blazing*（著火的）pines, like candles at an evening meeting.

"Bring forth the *converts*（改換信仰的人；變節者）!" cried a voice that echoed through the field and rolled into the forest.

At the word, Goodman Brown stepped forth from the shadow of the trees and approached the *congregation*（教友聚會）. He could have *sworn*（發誓）that his own dead father *beckoned*（招手）him to advance while a woman warned him back. Was it his mother? But he had no power to *retreat*（撤退；逃跑）one step, nor to *resist*（反抗）, even in thought.

"Welcome, my children," said the dark figure, "to the *communion*（通靈；交流）of your race. You have found thus your *nature*（本質）and your *destiny*（命運）."

"My children," said the figure, in a deep and *solemn tone*（莊嚴音調）, "Evil is the nature of mankind. Evil must be your only happiness. Welcome again, my children, to the communion of your race."

And there a *basin*（盆子）was in the rock. Did it contain water? or was it blood? Herein did the evil *dip*（沾水）his hand and lay the mark of *baptism*（受洗）upon their foreheads, that they might be *partakers*（伙伴）of their own. The husband cast one look at his pale wife, and Faith at him.

"Faith! Faith!" cried the husband, "look up to heaven, and resist the wicked one."

Whether Faith *obeyed*（守住）he knew not. The next morning young Goodman Brown came slowly into the street of Salem village, staring around him like a *bewildered*（迷失茫然）man.

Had Goodman Brown fallen asleep in the forest and only dreamed a wild dream of a *witch—meeting*（女巫的聚會）?

Since then, often, waking suddenly at midnight, he shrank from the *bosom of Faith*（自Faith的身軀退縮）; when the family *knelt down at prayer*（跪地祈福）, he *gazed sternly at*（嚴厲注視）his wife, and turned away. And when he had lived long, and was borne to his *grave*（墳墓）, they *carved*（雕刻）no *verse*（詩文）upon his *tombstone*（墓碑）, for his dying hour was *gloom*（幽暗；陰鬱的）.

四、作品延伸與作業

　　霍桑此文不論氣氛感受，不免讓人直覺聯想到歌德之〈浮士德〉善與惡的探討，又像是【聖經】的現代版〈約伯記〉，你對人性善與惡的兩元認為是邪不勝正？還是人性的相生相隨，無所謂對立？兩者任一的解釋，對人生現實世界的意義為何？

愛倫・坡《弗德馬先生案的真相》
——浪漫黑色劇之泰斗

小說特徵

驚悚、懸疑之「黑色浪漫主義」（Dark Romanticism）

埃德加・愛倫・玻
(Edgar Allan Poe, 1809 –1849)

Words have no power to impress the mind without the exquisite horror. I have no faith in human perfectability. Man is now not more happy- nor more wise, than he was 6000 years ago.

-Edgar Allan Poe

文字失去敏銳的恐懼，就沒有深印人心的力量。我對人性的完美沒有信心。比起六千年前，人是既沒更快樂，也沒更具智慧。

——愛倫・坡

一、作者短評

　　埃德加‧愛倫‧坡（Edgar Allan Poe），1809年，生於美國麻薩諸塞州波士頓，愛倫‧坡主要為其養父約翰愛倫（John Allan）所撫養長大，而將「愛倫」冠入其間，妻逝後，酗酒，生活潦倒，1849年10月7日，愛倫‧坡倒臥巴爾的摩溝壑之中，死因不明，得年才四十歲。

　　愛倫坡在他短暫四十歲生命中，作品思想鎖定人性陰暗面，視人生乃痛苦與恐懼之源，擅長描寫異想人格、犯罪心理、鬼魅、奇幻這類的題材，探討人類心靈最深層的陰鬱。小說情節充滿陰暗、恐怖、詭祕的氛圍，作品滿佈哀傷鬼魅，設計和鋪陳的技巧引人入勝，作品風格，奉為經典，歷久不衰，在美國文壇獨樹一格的地位。

　　愛倫‧坡結合驚悚與懸疑，所創作黑色浪漫小說，極具取悅大眾的高度趣味價值，幫助他被公認是推理、偵探小說之父。《莫爾格街兇殺案》（The Murders in the Rue Morgue,1841），不但被公認為史上的第一本推理小說，同時也是史上的第一宗密室殺人詭計（locked room mystery）。書中主角杜平（C. Auguste Dupin）也成小說世界裡的第一神探，成為許多後起仿傚的典範，最出名者莫過於日後之英國神探福爾摩斯，日本漫畫的柯南，尤其喜用第一人稱敘述案情，娓娓道來時的臨場感，根本是愛倫‧坡之翻版。

另外，當十九世紀人類科技，還沒有發達如今時，愛倫‧坡卻勇於走在時代的尖端，大量放入科幻的想像，又被視為科幻小說催生者。連今日的《阿凡達》導演詹姆士柯麥隆與史蒂芬史匹柏，亦望塵莫及，益增他作品可讀性的優勢。

二、作品分析

常有人問：「一個好的小說標準在那裏？」，答案見仁見智，莫衷一是；然排除個人主觀因素，或許我們可以求助於米蘭昆德拉在〈小說的藝術〉中，所提供「小說的四個召喚」，不失為評論小說的一個客觀方向：

（一）、夢的召喚：創意、創新性

（二）、思想的召喚：深度、深刻性

（三）、時間的召喚：感動、感人力量

（四）、遊戲的召喚：趣味、娛樂性

也就是說小說的高下，除滿足文學上，創意、深度的感動外，大眾市場的娛樂價值，也是重要的評量標準。至少，就最後一標準言，愛倫‧坡作品喜好以死亡和恐懼的主題特色，編撰謀殺、鬼魅、怪異劇情，所具高度驚異、創新之效果，帶領讀者進入人性最深的恐懼之中，常為市場暢銷之保證。

在《弗德馬先生案的真相》小說中，我們可以輕鬆的看出，它包含了所有艾倫‧坡創作想像的元素，主角是一名催眠師，希望運用催眠術於阻止死亡，而身患肺結核的弗德馬先生甘願成為主角的實驗對象，待弗德馬先生臨死前一刻，主角開始向他施行了催眠，弗德馬先生也果然在進入催眠狀態下死亡，但恐怖是，他卻能活著告訴催眠者自己已經死了，充滿了驚恐與異想的氣氛：

> *"Yes;—no;—I have been sleeping—and now—now—I am dead."*

弗德馬先生這種不生不死的狀態持了七個月，弗德馬先生看來也是不好受，終於接受喚醒的要求：

> *"For God's sake!—quick!—quick!—put me to sleep—or, quick!—waken me!—quick!—I say to you that I am dead!"*

主角終於向弗德馬先生解除催眠，弗德馬先生立即化為一灘臭水。可說是非常典型愛倫‧坡式的集科幻、想像與鬼魅於大成的小說之風。

三、閱讀文選

The Facts In The Case of M. Valdemar

Edgar Allan Poe

My *attention*（注意力）, for the last three years, had *been repeatedly drawn to*（一再被吸引到）the *subject*（主題）of *Mesmerism*（催眠術）and, about nine month ago, *it occurred to me*（一個…念頭進入腦海）a very *remarkable omission*（非常遺漏的事）—no person had as yet been mesmerized *in articulo mortis*（臨死時）.

When the ideas first occurred to me, it was of course natural that I should think of Ernest Valdemar. I spoke to him *frankly*（坦白地）upon the *subject*（主題）; and to my surprise, his interest seemed excited. He was a very thin, nervous man with white *whiskers*（落腮鬍）and black hair. He was *suffering from*（受苦於）*tuberculosis*（肺結核）. Sometimes, Valdemar spoke *calmly*（平靜地）of his *imminent*（即將的）death. He agreed to become the one for that *experiment*（實驗）. In fact, the *prospect*（想像；前途）excited him. Besides, he has no *relatives*（親戚）in America who would *object to*（反對）it.

One day Valdemar *submitted to*（接受）the experiment before his *demise*（死亡）. When I arrived at 7 p.m. Saturday for the experiment, Valdemar was so thin that his *cheekbones*（面頰

骨）showed through his skin. He *coughed*（咳嗽）frequently. His *pulse*（脈搏）was *faint*（薄弱）. *Nevertheless*（然而）, he *retained*（保有）mind and a *modicum of*（少量的）*physical strength*（生理力量）. Two doctors attended him. They *advised*（告知）me that Valdemar's disease had *ruined*（毀壞）his *lungs*（肺）. He would be expected to die at midnight Sunday. The doctors left but planed to return to check Valdemar at 10 p.m. Sunday.

While talking with Valdemar, I had second thoughts about the undertaking, for the only *witnesses*（見證者）to *observe*（觀察）it were a female nurse and a male nurse. So I waited until the following evening, by which time I had hired a medical student to witness the experiment and took notes. When I and the medical student arrive at 8 p.m., I went to work immediately.

I began by passing my hand over Valdemar's forehead, a technique I *previously*（先前）found successful in mesmerizing Valdemar. When the doctors arrive at 10 p.m., they permitted me to continue the experiment. After all, Valdemar will die very soon. Why not let me *proceed*（進行）?

At 10:55, Valdemar began *slipping into a trance*（進入昏迷狀態）. Over the next hour, I continued to work on him. At midnight, all present agreed that he was in *a perfect state of*（一完美的⋯狀態）mesmerism. One doctor, excited, decided to stay with Valdemar through the night; the other planed to return in the morning. The medical student and the nurses remained. At 3 a.m., I asked Valdemar whether he was asleep.

"Yes;—asleep now. Do not wake me!—let me die so!"

I questioned the "*sleep—waker*"（似睡似醒人）again, asking him whether he was in pain, because his *limbs*（四肢）were *rigid*（僵硬）.

"No pain—I am dying," Valdemar says.

When the other doctor arrived in the morning, he was *astonished*（驚訝）that Valdemar still alive. After *conferring*（商量）, the doctors said Valdemar should *remain*（仍然）in his present state until death, expected in minutes. I then asked Valdemar whether he was still sleeping. Immediately, Valdemar's eyes *rolled back*（翻開）, the skin turned white, the *circular spots*（圓形黑痣）on his cheeks disappeared, and *the lower jaw*（下顎）fell, *exposing*（露出）a black tongue.

So *hideous*（可怕；不忍卒睹）does he look that everyone stepped back from him. His tongue *vibrated*（顫動）, and in a minute they heard his voice. The sound seemed to come from a *cavern*（洞窟）deep in the earth. Valdemar then answered the question whether he was still sleeping :

"Yes;—no;—I have been sleeping —and now —now —I am dead."

The medical student *fainted*（昏倒）. The nurses left, refusing to return. After the doctors and I spent an hour trying to *revive*（救活）Valdemar, they observed that his breathing had stopped. However, Valdemar tried to answer questions but could not *articulate*（清楚的發音）. Meanwhile, at 10 a.m., Valdemar's *condition*（情況）was unchanged. But to awaken him, we believed, would be to lose him completely.

So he remained in his trance—for seven months. Nothing changes. Finally, the doctors and I agreed that their *only course*（唯一的路）is to try to awaken him. After I used mesmeric technique several times, the *iris*（瞳孔）of Valdemar's eye *emitted*（噴出）*a foul—smelling fluid*（一股惡臭的液汁）. I asked Valdemar to express his wishes.

"*For God's sake!*（看在老天份上）—quick!—quick!—put me to sleep—or, quick!—waken me!—quick!—I say to you that I am dead! "

As I rapidly made the mesmeric passes, amid *ejaculations*（突然的喊叫）of "dead! dead! " absolutely *bursting from*（自…爆出）the tongue and not from the lips of the sufferer, his whole *frame*（身體；骨架）at once *crumbled*（瞬間潰散）—*rotted away*（腐爛）beneath my hands. Upon the bed, there lay a nearly *liquid mass of detestable putrescence*（一團噁心的腐敗膿水）.

四、作品延伸作業

　　愛倫‧坡除以娛樂通俗恐怖小說知名外，他也是位傑出的詩人，其詩以美著稱，由於陰暗的性格，他認為世上最淒美者莫過於一個淑女的死亡，愛倫坡稱之為「世上最富詩意的話題」。特選其Annabel Lee，詩中男子悼念他死去的愛人，不僅詩的內容美，音韻也美。詩中如魅如幻，深刻動人，可以說是美到極致，別有意境。

Annabel Lee

It was many and many a year ago,

In a kingdom by the sea,

That a maiden there lived whom you may know

By the name of Annabel Lee;

And this maiden she lived with no other thought

Than to love and be love by me.

She was a child and I was a child,

In this kingdom by the sea,

But we loved with a love that was more than love

I and my Annabel Lee —

With a love that the winged seraphs of Heaven

Coveted her and me.

And this was the reason that, long ago,

In this kingdom by the sea,

A wind blew out of cloud by night

Chilling my Annabel Lee;

So that her highborn kinsmen came

And bore her away from me,

To shut her up in a sepulcher

In this kingdom by the sea.

那是多年多年以前的事

一個濱海的王國裡

住著一位你可能認識的姑娘

名叫 安娜貝‧李

她生命別無心思

唯與我相愛相依

她是個孩子 而我也是

在這個濱海的王國裡

我們超越愛情的愛來相愛

我與我的 安娜貝‧李之愛

連六翼天使（天使位階最高者）

也垂涎不已

正因此故 在幽遠的從前

在這個濱海的王國裡

一陣風夜間自雲中吹起

冷冽了我 心愛的 安娜貝‧李

於是她那高貴的親屬 降臨凡地

硬生生的把我倆拆離

將她囚禁在墳穴裡

就在這濱海的王國裡

The angels, not half so happy in Heaven,

Went envying her and me:

Yes! that was the reason

(as all men know, In this kingdom by the sea)

That the wind came out of the cloud, chilling

And killing my Annabel Lee.

But our love it was stronger by far than the love

Of those who were older than we —

Of many far wiser than we —

And neither the angels in Heaven above,

Nor the demons down under the sea,

Can ever dissever my soul from the soul

Of the beautiful Annabel Lee:

For the moon never beams without bringing me dreams

Of the beautiful Annabel Lee

And the stars never rise but I see the bright eyes

Of the beautiful Annabel Lee;

And so, all the night—tide, I lie down by the side

Of my darling, my darling, my life and my bride.

In the sepulchre there by the sea —

In her tomb by the side of the sea.

天使 在天堂裡的歡愉勝不過我們

因而對我倆心生妒忌

是的！就是這緣故！

（在濱海的王國裡，人人都知悉）

就是這陣雲端的寒風，冷厲的

奪走我的安娜貝‧李

可是 我們的愛更濃烈了

遠勝於我們的長者

更勝於我們的先哲

無論是天上的天使

或是海底的水妖

都無法將我倆的靈魂分離

我與我美麗的安娜貝的靈魂

只因月輝照映必引領我

進入有安娜貝的美麗夢境裡

只因：每當星光冉升 我定看見

安娜貝 她那晶瑩雙眸的深帶

於是漫漫夜潮裡 我都與她相徘

我的愛 我的生命我的新娘

在傍海的墓穴棲息

在滄海之濱的墓園裡

5 赫爾曼‧梅爾維爾《提琴手》 ——人性宿命式悲劇

小說特徵

人性宿命、宗教、象徵主義

赫爾曼‧梅爾維爾
(Herman Melville, 1819 –1891)

With genius and without fame, he is happier than a king.

-Herman Melville

一個沒有榮耀的天才，他比國王更快樂。

——赫爾曼‧梅爾維爾

一、作者短評

　　赫爾曼・梅爾維爾，1819年，出生於紐約。十三歲時，父親經商失敗破產，留下一家九口，於是梅爾維爾自十五歲，就輟學開始外出工作。1839年起，梅爾維爾成為捕鯨船水手，航行於南太平洋一帶，曾在南太平洋群島被食人族所俘虜，脫逃後，1846年，他根據這一經歷，發表《提比》（Typee）小說，隔年又發表《渥姆》（Omoo）也是《提比》的續集。

　　1850年，他以其海上捕鯨的經歷為事實，開始創作《白鯨記》（Moby—Dick），前後花了17個月，1851年夏完稿，同年出版。梅爾維爾《白鯨記》這部小說日後被認為是美國最偉大的小說之一，但第一年竟然只賣出5本，在當時非但沒有引起轟動，反惹來許多的非議，使他十分失望。他的作品還包括短篇小說，如《書記員巴特子比》（1856年）以及中篇小說《比利・巴德》（1924年出版）。梅爾維爾生前默默無聞，晚年轉而寫詩，出版商拒絕繼續讓他預支稿費，他曾寫信給霍桑：「激動我的心靈，促使我寫作的東西，我寫不成了——因為它無利可圖。可是要我改弦更張，不這麼寫，我辦不到。」1891年9月28日，梅爾維爾過世於紐約，以窮途潦倒終。

　　《白鯨記》直到出版後七十年，才獲得重視。英國作家毛姆在《世界十大小說家及其代表作》一書中對《白鯨記》的評價遠在美國其他作家愛倫・坡與馬克吐溫之上。

二、作品分析

就代表美國本土浪漫文學之超越主義作品內容來看，大部都是對個人精神作光明面的推揚；人性本善，所以個人的感性判斷總是成功、美滿；個人的選擇，也往往是以喜劇結局。但超越主義作家中，也不乏對人性力量做反面悲觀思考的創作，形成美國文學藝術中另股主流。最出名除霍桑外，梅爾維爾則屬另一代表。兩人代表之作《紅字》與《白鯨記》中，兩書的主角：無論是赫斯特或阿巴船長，最終都無法抗拒清教枷鎖與白鯨的吞噬，暗喻人性中不可改變的宿命式悲劇。

在小說寫作上，梅爾維爾深受莎士比亞與霍桑的啟發與影響最大，一心以兩人為效法對象，梅爾維爾認為莎士比亞之所以能為莎士比亞，乃在於他能刻畫生活的醜惡面，而梅爾維爾視霍桑是最好的朋友，也在他發現霍桑的作品中，具有莎士比亞一樣的特質，曾說：「吸引我並使入迷的是霍桑作品中所表現的醜陋面。」，梅爾維爾深愛霍桑的小說《紅字》。同樣，當梅爾維爾1850年2月，埋首《白鯨記》的寫作時，梅爾維爾寫信給霍桑說：「我寫了一本邪書，不過，我覺得像羔羊一般潔白無疵。」霍桑手邊曾有一本梅爾維爾致贈的《白鯨記》，梅爾維爾和霍桑的創作皆帶有宗教神秘和悲觀的色彩，霍桑深受清教的影響，梅爾維爾喜讀聖經，他《白鯨記》有可能來自聖經中約拿（Jonah）拒絕接受上帝召喚，企圖坐船逃跑，而被上帝所派的鯨魚吞到肚中的啟發，梅爾維爾也效法霍桑，喜好象徵手法的運用，書中的白鯨宛如自然界無法抗拒的力量，有如人生命運的譬喻，船長阿巴（Ahab）的「注定失敗，仍要奮鬥」的追捕白鯨，最後卻反為白鯨所噬，充滿叛逆英雄的悲劇性，暗喻個人自我實現的堅持，不只是個人的解放，也會是自我毀滅。

本書所選梅爾維爾的短篇小說《提琴手》，全文簡潔明快，藉著一位沒有天份，卻汲營於虛名的悲憤作家和一位具有天份，卻又放棄一切名利，卻滿足自在提琴家的故事，告訴人有沒有天賦或名氣，不是決定你人生滿意與否的主因，個人的快樂跟他們是沒有太大的關係，人生其實是有捨才有得，放手反而才能擁有。

三、閱讀文選

The Fiddler

Herman Melville

So my *poem*（詩）is *damned*（該死；糟糕）, and *immortal fame*（不朽名聲）is not for me! I am nobody forever and ever. *Intolerable fate!*（無情的命運！）

Snatching（一把抓住）my hat, I *dashed down the criticism*（丟下評論）, and *rushed out into*（快速跑去）Broadway, where I met my old friend Standard.

"Well met, Helmstone , my boy! Ah! what's the matter? Haven't been *committing murder*（犯了謀殺案）? You look wild! "

"You have seen it then? " said I, of course *referring to*（意指） the criticism.

"Oh yes; I was there at the morning *circus performance*（馬戲 班表演）. Great *clown*（小丑）, I *assure*（保證）you. But here comes Hautboy. Hautboy—Helmstone. "

I *gazed on*（凝視）the face of the new acquaintance. His person was short and full, with a *juvenile cast*（少年的氣質）to it. His hair alone *betrayed*（暴露）that he was not an *overgrown*（早 熟的）boy. From his hair I set him down as forty or more.

"Come, Standard," he happily cried to my friend, "are you not going to the circus? The clown is *inimitable*（獨一無二的）, they say. Come; Mr. Helmstone, too—come both; and circus over, we'll take a nice *stew*（燉菜）and *punch*（酒的一種）at Taylor's. "

During the circus performance I kept my eye more on Hautboy than on the celebrated clown. Hautboy was the sight for me. In a man of forty I saw a boy of twelve; and this too without the *slightest abatement*（絲毫不減）of my respect. Because all was so honest and natural, every *expression and attitude*（外表與態度）so *graceful*（優雅的）with *genuine*（真實的）*good—nature*（善 良）. Such genuine enjoyment as his *struck me to the soul*（讓我靈 魂感受）with a sense of the reality of the thing called happiness.

But much as I gazed upon Hautboy, and as much as I *admired* （仰慕）his air, yet that *desperate mood*（絕望情緒）in which I had first rushed from the house had not so entirely *departed*（離 去）. Again my eyes *swept*（掃過）the circus, and fell on the *countenance*（表情）of Hautboy. But its clear honest cheeriness disdained my disdain. My intolerant pride was *rebuked*（斥退）. *At the very instant I felt the dart of the censure*（每當我起批評的衝動）, his eye *twinkled*（閃爍）, his hand waved, his voice was in *jubilant delight*（充滿喜悅）at another joke of the clown.

Circus over, we went to Taylor's. Among crowds of others, we sat down to our stews and punches at one of the small marble tables. Hautboy sat opposite to me. As the conversation proceeded between Standard and him, I was more and more struck with his excellent judgment. What was sad in the world he did not *superficially gainsay*（膚淺地否定）; what was glad in it he did not *cynically slur*（憤世嫉俗地中傷）. He but acknowledged facts.

Suddenly remembering an *engagement*（約定）, he took up his hat, bowed pleasantly, and left us.

"Well, Helmstone," said Standard, "what do you think of your *new acquaintance*（新朋友）？"

"New acquaintance indeed," echoed I. "I hugely love and admire him, Standard. I wish I were Hautboy."

"Ah? That's a pity, now. There's only one Hautboy in the world."

This last remark somehow *revived*（復活）my *dark mood*（負面的情緒）.

"His wonderful cheerfulness, I suppose," said I, *sneering with spleen*（帶有惡意的嘲諷）, " Unpossessed of genius, Hautboy is blessed（Hautboy是受眷顧的，但不是天才）."

"Ah? You would not think him an genius, then？"

"Genius? What! such a short, fat fellow a genius！"

"Ah? You speak very decidedly."

"Yes, Standard," cried I, increasing in spleen, "your *cheery*（快活有精神的）Hautboy, after all, is no *pattern*（典範）for you and me. With *average*（平庸的）abilities; passions *docile*（溫馴），

—how can your Hautboy be made a reasonable example to a *handy*（靈巧；高明）fellow like you, or an ambitious dreamer like me?

"Did you ever hear of Master Betty? "

"The great English *prodigy*（天才；神童）! What can Master Betty, the great English genius boy twelve years old *have to do with*（與……有關）the poor Hautboy, an American of forty? Besides, Master Betty must be dead and buried long. "

A sudden noise at my side attracted my ear. Turning, I saw Hautboy again, who reseated himself on the chair he had left.

"I was behind time with my engagement," said Hautboy, "so I would run back and rejoin you. But come, you have sat long enough here. Let us go to my rooms. It is only a five minutes' walk."

"If you will promise to fiddle for us, we will," said Standard.

"I will gladly fiddle," replied Hautboy to Standard. "Come on."

In a few minutes we found ourselves in the fifth story of a sort of storehouse, in Broadway. It was curiously furnished with all sorts of odd and *old—fashioned*（奇怪過時的）furniture. But all was charmingly clean and *cozy*（溫暖舒適）.

Pressed by Standard, Hautboy got out his *dented*（破舊的）old fiddle and, sitting down on a *tall rickety stool*（搖晃的高腳椅）, played away right merrily. But common as were the tunes, I was *transfixed*（呆楞）by something miraculous in the style. All my *moody discontent*（不滿情緒）, every *vestige of peevishness fled*（焦躁的形跡離去）. My whole *splenetic soul capitulated to*（惡念的靈魂，投降於）the magical fiddle.

The fiddle ceased. Once more, with redoubled curiosity, I gazed upon the easy, *indifferent*（冷默的）Hautboy.

When, leaving him, Standard and I were in the street once more.

"You *mock*（嘲弄）me, Standard. There is some mystery here.

Tell me, I entreat you, who is Hautboy?"

"An *extraordinary*（卓越不凡的）genius, Helmstone," said Standard, " One who has been an object of *wonder*（驚議的奇才）to the wisest. But today he walks Broadway and no man knows him. He who has a hundred times been *crowned with laurels*（桂冠加冕；喻名氣）, now wears, as you see, a *bunged beaver*（笨拙的厚呢）. Once *fortune poured showers of gold into his lap*（錢淹腳目）, today, from house to house, teaching fiddling for a living. With genius and without fame, he is happier than a king. "

"His true name? "

"Let me whisper it in your ear."

"What! Oh, Standard, myself, as a child, have *shouted myself hoarse*（喊到嘶啞的）*applauding*（鼓掌讚賞）that very name."

"I have heard your poem was not very *handsomely*（大方普遍地）received," said Standard .

"Shall not my *petty affair*（微不足道的小事）be as nothing, when I behold in Hautboy?"

Next day I tore all my *manuscripts*（稿紙）, bought me a fiddle, and went to take regular lessons of Hautboy.

四、作品延伸作業

梅爾維爾一生反抗威權體制，抗議生存制度，代表作品《白鯨記》，書中船長阿巴（Ahab）瘋狂的追捕白鯨，一付沒到手，絕不放手的決心，彷彿反射梅爾維爾堅持到底的心態，但由《提琴手》一文，那位悲憤作家Helmstone羨慕放棄名利，滿足自在提琴家Hautboy，是表達梅爾維爾心態的轉變嗎？

狄更斯《兒童的故事》
——資本社會的人道寫實先驅

小說特徵

資本社會的負面現象：貧富
差距、都市、監獄問題

查爾斯・狄更斯
(Charles Dickens, 1812 –1870)

This is the best of the time, this is the worst of the time.
-Charles Dickens, A Tale of Two Cities

這是最好的時刻，也是最壞的時刻。

——查爾斯・狄更斯《雙城記》

一、作者短評

狄更斯，1812年，出生於英格蘭樸次茅斯，父親約翰・狄更斯因舉債不還被捕下獄，一家人隨著父親遷至牢房居住，狄更斯也因此被送到倫敦一家鞋油店，每天工作10個小時。或許是由於這段經歷，備嚐艱辛、屈辱，看盡人情冷暖，使得狄更斯的作品更關注底層社會的生活狀態。

狄更斯並沒有接受很多的正規教育，是靠自學成才。狄更斯後來成為《晨報》的國會記者，專門採訪英國下議院的政策辯論，也時常環遊英倫採訪各種選舉活動。狄更斯前往他所嚮往的美國，他在美國的見聞被收進1842年出版的《美國紀行》，並在美國享有極大的聲望及影響力，可以說美國十九世紀以後，批判資本社會黑暗的小說，無不受狄更斯的啟發與繼承。

1849年他出版了自傳題材的小說《塊肉餘生錄》，這部小說的內容與狄更斯的個人經歷有很大關係，是狄更斯的代表作。狄更斯以後的小說顯得更為尖銳並具批判性，著名的有《雙城記》。

狄更斯一生刻苦勤勉，繁重的勞動和現實改革的失望，嚴重損害了他的健康。1870年6月9日狄更斯因腦溢血與世長辭，被安葬在西敏寺，他的墓碑上如此寫道：「他是貧窮、受苦與被壓迫人民的同情者；他的去世令世界失去了一位偉大的作家。」

二、作品分析

英國至維多利亞時期（1819—1891），靠工業革命之助，國力雖達鼎盛，人民貧富差距拉大，造成「兩個國度的問題」（The issue of two nations），社會運動乘勢而起。影響於文學者，也宣告英國浪漫主義文學結束，也因此，狄更斯的小說總是揭露工業社會中，弱勢小民生活的苦楚與不公，筆觸描繪單調的工業時代，冷漠疏離、功利至上的社會，他將社會正義的意識置入文學，制衡十九世紀資本文明越來越窄化人性的問題，是狄更斯對小說的最大貢獻。而狄更斯的寫實主義，專事揭露社會階層與貧窮的作品，也成了英國維多利亞時期最有代表性作家。

狄更斯《兒童的故事》敘述了一位旅人途中，見證一名兒童自少年、青年、紳士到老年的一步步成長，旅人並在每一階段，陪他玩樂、學習、工作，再看他成家、生子、立業，最後歸於塵土。簡單的描述所有人的一生段落不過如此，生命就是如此的單調與滿足，宛如一幅人生畫卷。狄更斯也碰觸了死亡的探討，他將人生的每一個階段的結束—如兒童到少年，不一定是死亡，其實是另段的開始，不需如旅人那般的失落及驚訝，即便到了盡頭，生命的過程也是延續的，在這接力的過程中，我們不過是其中的一位接棒人罷了！

三、閱讀文選

The Child's Story

Charles Dickens

Once upon a time, a good many years ago, there was a traveler, and he set out upon a journey. It was a *magic journey*（魔幻的旅程）.

He travelled along a rather dark *path*（道路）for some little time, without meeting anything, until at last he came to a beautiful child. So he said to the child, "What do you do here?" And the child said, "I am always at play. Come and play with me!"

So, he played with that child, the whole day long, and they were very merry. The sky was so blue, the sun was so bright, the water was so sparkling, the leaves were so green, and the flowers were so lovely, that everything was beautiful. When it rained, they loved to watch the falling drops, and to smell the fresh *scents*（香味）. When it *blew*（吹風）, it was *delightful*（愉悅的）to listen to the wind. But, when it snowed, that was best of all; for, they liked nothing so well as to look up at the white flakes falling fast and thick, like down from the *breasts*（胸口）of millions of white birds; and to see *how smooth and deep the drift*（白雪輕滑下沉的飄浮）was.

But, one day, of a sudden, the traveler lost the child. He called to him over and over again, but got no answer. So, he went upon his road, until at last he came to a handsome boy. So, he said to the boy, "What do you do here?" And the boy said, "I am always learning. Come and learn with me."

So he learned with that boy about the Greeks and the Romans, and learned more than I could tell. But, they were not always learning; they had the *merriest*（最快樂的）games that ever were played. They *rowed*（划船）upon the river in summer, and skated on the ice in winter; they were *active on horseback*（活躍馬背上）; at *cricket*（板球）, and more sports; nobody could beat them.

Still, one day, in the midst of all these pleasures, the traveler lost the boy as he had lost the child, and, after calling to him *in vain*（無效）, went on upon his journey, until at last he came to a young man. So, he said to the young man, "What do you do here?" And the young man said, "I am always in love. Come and love with me."

So, he went away with that young man, and they came to one of the prettiest girls that ever was seen— Fanny. So, the young man fell in love directly. Well! they *quarreled*（爭吵）sometimes ,and they *made it up*（和好）, and they sat in the dark, and wrote letters every day, and were *engaged*（訂婚）at Christmas-time, and sat close to one another by the fire, and were going to be married very soon.

But, the traveler lost them one day, as he had lost *the rest of*（其餘的）his friends, and went on upon his journey, until at last he came to a middle-aged gentleman. So, he said to the gentleman, "What are you doing here?" And his answer was, "I am always busy. Come and be busy with me!"

So, he began to be very busy with that gentleman. The gentleman was not alone, but had a lady of about the same age with him, who was his Wife; and they had children, who were with them too. They all went on together.

At last, there had been so many *partings*（分離）. One of the children said, "Father, I am going to sea," and another said, "Father, I am going to India," and another, "Father, I am going to seek my fortune where I can," and another, "Father, I am going to Heaven!"

There were no children left, and only the gentleman, and the lady, went forward on their journey when the lady stopped.

"My husband," said the lady. "I am called."

They listened, and they heard a voice a long way down the *avenue*（大道）, say, "Mother, mother!"

The father said, "I pray not yet. The sunset is very near. I pray not yet!"

Then, the mother kissed him, and said, "My dearest, I am *summoned*（蒙主恩召）, and I go!" And she was gone. And the traveler and he were left alone together.

Yet, once more, the traveler lost his friend. He called and called, but there was no reply, and he came to an old man sitting on a fallen tree. So, he said to the old man, "What do you do here?" And the old man said with a calm smile, "I am always remembering. Come and remember with me!"

So the traveler sat down by the side of that old man, face to face with the *serene*（平靜的）sunset; and all his friends came softly back and stood around him. The beautiful child, the handsome boy, the young man in love, the father, mother, and children: every one of them was there, and he had lost nothing.

四、作品延伸作業

在今年，狄更斯正滿200生辰的時候。資本社會制度，相較以往，已至控制人民生活的目標下，再讀狄更斯《兒童的故事》，他對人生旅程的必然性，所表達的涵義，是消極？淡定？抑無法改變？你以為如何？

7

安布魯・畢爾斯《梟河橋記事》
——扭曲時空、真實謊言的創意

安布魯・畢爾斯
Ambrose G. Bierce（1842－1913）

🖋 **小說特徵**
戰爭與超自然手法的技巧

..... he feels a stunning blow upon the back of the neck; a blinding white light blazes all about him —then all is darkness and silence!
 Peyton Farquhar was dead; his body, with a broken neck, swung gently from side to side beneath the timbers of the Owl Creek bridge.

-Ambrose G. Bierce, An Occurrence at Owl Creek Bridge

他突然感到頸項被猛然一擊，四周發出灼熱目眩的白光，然後一切歸於黑暗、寂靜。Peyton Farquhar死了，斷了頸項的屍體在梟河橋下來回地盪來盪去。

——安布魯・畢爾斯《梟河橋記事》

一、作者短評

安布魯·畢爾斯（Ambrose Bierce），1842年，出生於俄亥俄州，成長在印地安那州，在美國兩地當時雖是中西部尚未開化拓荒之地，但畢爾斯遺傳父母文學喜好，也愛上寫作。1861年美國南北內戰爆發，畢爾斯隨即加入了北方部隊，在他服役的四年間，戰場的廝殺，使他頭部曾嚴重受傷，最後以少校軍銜退役。戰後，畢爾斯專職於舊金山報社擔任報紙專欄作家，由於文風嘲諷，讓他贏得「辛辣畢爾斯（Bitter Bierce）」之封號。

畢爾斯的小說多以親身參與之美國內戰為題材，並由戰爭探索人性的旨味。他許多傑出的短篇故事都是以南北戰爭的恐怖經驗為主題，細節寫實逼真，加上畢爾斯是講述超自然故事的能手，這將戰場結合靈異想像的創作，結局常現毛骨悚然及驚駭高潮效果，《梟河橋記事》（An Occurrence at Owl Creek Bridge）公認是此絕佳之範例。

畢爾斯晚年深受戰時受傷後遺症與氣喘之苦。1913年，畢爾斯前往墨西哥，想要獨家採訪當地革命叛亂，從此，音信杳然，據信是被叛軍所害，成為美國最出名的文學家失蹤案例之一。

二、作品分析

在許榮哲先生之〈小說課〉提到，一般小說的敘事流程，都是基於事實的前提，引領讀者進入一步步安排的情節，最後在真相答案的揭曉下，畫下結局。但是，想像一下，如果你發現引領你進入故事的敘事者，從頭到尾都在說謊，結果你不但不氣憤，反而感動？可會是什麼的小說創意情況。在畢爾斯的《梟河橋記事》就提供了此一類屬的小說典範，內容敘述：南軍士兵Peyton Farquhar被北軍俘虜，綁在鐵橋上要吊死時，Farquhar正在作最後妻小的懷想時，意外發生了，繩索斷裂，Farquhar掉到河裏，展開他一連串的「回家」逃亡，他掙扎出漩渦激流的吞噬，閃過追捕他的槍林彈雨，艱苦上岸，馬不停啼地跑了一天一夜，他又累又餓，但一想到妻子，馬上又加緊腳步，最後Farquhar終於回到了家，眼見美麗的妻子在晨光明朗的家門口迎接，就要抱住她時…。目前為止，畢爾百分之九十九的內容，都集中描述Farquhar在戰爭中死亡的恐懼，並交纏著他求生與再見妻子的饑渴，終於，當所有人正感動主角與妻子團聚時，令人驚心恐怖的高峰，卻在終了的百分之一，瞬間畫下：

「他突然感到項頸被猛然一擊，四周發出灼熱目眩的白光，然後一切歸於暗、寂靜。Peyton Farquhar死了，斷了項頸的屍體在梟溪橋下來回地盪來蕩去。」

畢爾斯只管寫出主角心靈的渴望，不顧時空、生理的物理限制，看到了不存在的「身體逃亡」，而不是選擇以「靈魂的逃亡」的鬼片方式處理，正因為主角強烈要回家見他妻子最後一面，所以他回家不但合理，只要人同此心，儘管真相是一切都沒有發生，小說不但可以不必向科學負責，還讓讀者感動、叫好。畢爾斯此一扭曲時空、真實謊言的創意，從此蔚為風行，成了小說、電影創作的法寶，前些時，由布魯斯威利斯所主演電影《神鬼第六感》、妮可基曼《靈異第六感》、《蘇西的世界》，國片周杰倫《不能說的秘密》，都是基於此一構想的作品。

三、閱讀文選：

An Occurrence at Owl Creek Bridge

Ambrose Bierce

A man stood upon a railroad bridge in northern Alabama, looking down into the *swift*（快速的）water twenty feet below. The man's hands were behind his back, the *wrists*（手腕）*bound*（綁縛）with a *cord*（細繩）. *A rope closely encircled his neck*（繩索緊繞脖上）. It was his *executioners*（死刑）—two *soldiers*（士兵）of the *Federal army*（北軍）, directed by a *sergeant*（士官）. *At a short remove*（不遠距離）upon the same *temporary platform*（臨時高檯上）was an officer *in uniform*（軍服）. He is a *captain*（上尉）.

The man to *be hanged*（吊死）was Peyton Farquhar, who was a *well—to—do planter*（富裕的大農場主人）, of an old and highly respected Alabama family. He was apparently about thirty-five years of age. His *features*（五官；臉部）were good—a straight nose, firm mouth, broad forehead, from which his long, dark hair was *combed straight back*（向後直線梳理）, falling behind his ears.

The preparations was complete. At a *signal*（信號）from the captain, the *plank*（厚板）upon which the *condemned*（定罪的）man had been standing would be *drawn away*（拉開）and go down. His face had not been covered nor his eyes *bandaged*（包起來）. He let *his gaze wander*（他的目光徘徊）to the *swirling water*（漩渦）of the *stream*（河流）racing madly beneath his feet.

He closed his eyes in order to fix his last thoughts upon his wife and children. The *intervals of silence*（安靜的間隔）grew longer, the delays became *maddening*（令人發瘋）. What he heard was the *ticking*（滴答聲）of his watch.

He unclosed his eyes and saw again the water below him. "If I could free my hands," he thought, "I might throw off the *noose*（吊人索）and *spring into*（跳入）the stream. By *diving*（潛水）I could *evade*（躲開）the bullets and, swimming *vigorously*（活力有精神地）, *reach the bank*（河岸）, take to the woods and get away home."

As these thoughts were *flashed into*（閃過）the *doomed*（注定該死的）man's brain, the captain gave the signal.

As Peyton Farquhar fell straight downward the bridge he lost *consciousness*（知覺）. He was awakened—*ages*（數世紀）later, it seemed to him—by the pain of a *sharp pressure*（痛楚的壓迫）upon his throat, followed by a sense of *suffocation*（窒息）. His neck ached horribly; his brain was on fire; his heart was almost out of his mouth. His *chest*（胸膛）*expanded*（擴張）, and his *lungs engulfed a great draught of air*（肺陷入大量缺氧）, *he expelled in a shriek*（大叫出聲）！

Then all at once, the power of thought was *restored*（回復）; he knew that the rope had broken and he had fallen into the stream.

There was no *strangulation*（絞死）; he was trying to free his hands. The noose fell away; his arms parted and *floated*（漂浮）upward. He opened his eyes in the darkness and saw above him a *gleam*（微光）of light, but how distant, *how inaccessible*（遙不可及）! Then it began to grow and brighten, and he knew that he was rising toward the *surface*（水面）.

He was now in full possession of his *physical*（生理的）senses. He had come to the *surface*（水面）, and he saw the soldiers upon the bridge, the captain, the sergeant, the two soldiers, his executioners. He saw one of the *sentinels*（衛兵）with his rifle at his shoulder, something struck the water within a few inches of his head, *spattering*（濺潑）his face with *spray*（水花）, added with what fell those *cruel*（殘酷的）words:

"Attention, company! . . Shoulder arms! . . . Ready! . . . *Aim*（瞄準）! . . . Fire!"

Farquhar *dived*（潛水）as deeply as he could. As he rose to the surface, he was farther down stream nearer to safety. The two sentinels fired again, independently and ineffectually. The *cannon*（大砲）had taken a hand in the game. A rising sheet of water *curved over*（高高捲起）him, fell down upon him, blinded him, strangled him!

He *sprang to*（跳起）his feet, *rushed up the sloping bank*（衝上坡岸）. He *dug*（挖掘）his fingers into the sand, which looked like diamonds, *rubies*（紅寶石）, *emeralds*（翡翠）; he could think of nothing beautiful which it did not *resemble*（類似）and *plunged into*（鑽入）the forest.

All that day he traveled. The forest seemed *interminable*（無止盡的）; nowhere did he discover a break in it, not even a woodman's road. By nightfall he was *fatigued*（疲憊）, footsore, *famishing*（饑餓）. The thought of his wife and children urged him on. His neck was in pain where the rope had *bruised*（瘀傷）it. His tongue was *swollen*（腫脹）with thirst. At last he found a road which led him in what he knew to be the right direction. It was as wide and straight as a city street. He *distinctly*（清楚地）heard *whispers*（耳語聲）in an *familiar tongue*（熟悉的話語）.

He stands at the *gate*（大門）of his own home. All is as he left it, and all bright and beautiful in the morning sunshine. As he pushes open the gate, his wife, looking fresh and cool and sweet, steps down from the *veranda*（陽台）to meet him. Ah, how beautiful she is! He springs forward with extended arms. As he is about to *clasp*（擁抱）her he feels a *stunning blow upon*（令人昏眩的重扯）the back of the neck; *a blinding white light blazes*（一道目眩的白燄烈光）all about him——then all is darkness and silence!

Peyton Farquhar was dead; his body, with a broken neck, swung gently from side to side beneath the timbers of the Owl Creek bridge.

四、作品延伸作業

你能找出一部鬼片，改以「真實謊言」的模式製作，呈現不同更佳的效果？

8 傑克‧倫敦《生火》
——自然中的人性原始力

傑克‧倫敦
(Jack London, 1876 –1916)

✒ **小說特徵**

自然主義與社會達爾文思想
的人性衝突

The trouble with him was that he was without imagination.

-Jack London, "To Build A Fire"

人最大的麻煩就是沒有想像力。

——傑克‧倫敦 《生火》

一、作者短評

　　傑克・倫敦（Jack London），1876年，出生於美國加州舊金山。自童年起，傑克・倫敦便飽嘗了貧困的滋味，靠自學，當童工維生。1890年，倫敦滿14歲，雖然脫離童工限制，進入罐頭廠工作，但一天10小時工作，而每小時的工資不超過10分；之後，傑克・倫敦失業，輾轉流浪於美國和加拿大各大都市的貧民窟。

　　1890年，美國資本主義與達爾文理論的無縫接軌結合，表面是「公平競爭，自由放任」的高尚動人，實則是冷血現實地奉「弱肉強食，適者生存」為當時金科玉律。這也促成自幼苦嚐美國資本家剝削殘酷的傑克・倫敦成為鬥志昂揚的社會主義信徒，熱心美國工人運動，倫敦在公共圖書館學習達爾文、馬克思、尼采的著作，他用一年的時間學完了中學4年的課程，順利考入位於伯克利的加州大學，但四個月後，就被學校退學，倫敦前往阿拉斯加淘金，旅程中的經歷和觀察，幫助他寫下了美國文學史上的經典之作《野性的呼喚》（The Call of the Wild）與稍後的《狼牙》（White Fang）：敘述一隻狼狗逐漸習慣人類世界，最後甚至犧牲性命以挽救主人生命的感人故事。

　　傑克・倫敦從小就對動物懷有深厚的感情，所創作一系列的冒險小說，狼犬自然成了他作品不可或缺的主角，《生火》可視為《野性的呼喚》姐妹篇。這一系列由冰天雪地、旅人與狼犬所組合的求生探險卡司，兼顧自然與寫實主義的手法，旅途中，人與自然以及人與狗之間情節，構成傑克倫敦小說的「北國法典」（London's Code of Northland），人類如野獸般掙扎求生的內容，看似與達爾文的「弱肉強食，適者生存」呼應，實則隱喻資本主義社會的殘酷無情和對金錢的崇拜，讓人性之同情心和無私變成了血腥慾望，沒有互助與奉獻，這種殘酷法典之最終結局便是自我毀滅。

傑克·倫敦在1916年11月22日，離世，據信是服用過量麻醉藥品自殺。

二、作品分析

傑克倫敦創作目的與動機，深受1890年代美國資本主義社會背景下，一生苦澀經驗大有關係：由於美國資本主義思想產生，基礎是混合了美國清教「工作倫理」（work ethics）之傳統信仰、工商革命的擴張現實，加以達爾文「適者生存」理論與美式民主的全面結合助陣；財富成為衡量一個人的標準，資本家如「鋼鐵大王」卡內基或「石油大王」洛克斐勒代表了人生成功的典範，這時顛沛流離的傑克倫敦則成了社會定義下的失敗者。

傑克倫敦代表作《生火》是以一個北國凍原的危險旅程而鋪展，描寫一個旅人過度自信的研判路線下，闖入暴風雪，先是雙腳踏入伏冰下的積水，又誤判形勢在樹下生火求生，眼看火苗終於生了起來，旅人正要鬆口氣之際，火苗熱氣上升，溶化了樹枝上的一堆積雪，雪掉落下來，把火堆澆息，待生火再度失敗，旅人已喪失求生意志，便乾脆坐著等死。其實，小說重點不在於主角的最後凍死，而在於他對事物的本質認識不當，付出生命的代價。

倫敦筆下，酷寒不過是一個象徵人類所不能察覺經驗範疇的暗喻，而人在大自然裡，注重官能、講究理性，以現實為引導，眼光的短淺，而萎縮了古老、難以言諭的本能引導。當旅人生火求生一再的失誤，他自以為是的智能是無用武之地，相反地，狗的本能就佔了優勢。這也是傑克倫敦好用的敘事手法，表面描寫人與動物、人與環境的抗爭，實則表達人與動物在大自然生存抗爭的那種原始慾望與動能，每個故事都有他親身經歷，方能有如此身歷其境的貼切，表現出他自然主義寫作的粗獷風格與自然無情的悲劇性，隱含了對社會正義及弱勢的關切，揭示資本社會有如冰原世界的冷漠與無情。

To Build A Fire

Jack London

Day had broken cold and *gray*（灰色）, *exceedingly*（過度地）cold and gray. It was nine o'clock. There was no sun nor a cloud in the sky. The man *flung*（拋向…）a look back along the way he had come. It was all pure white. North and south, as far as his eye could see, it was unbroken white, *save for*（除了）a dark hair—line *horizon*（地平線）.

He was a newcomer in the land. The trouble with him was that he was without imagination. He was quick and *alert in*（警覺到）the things of life, but only in the things, and not in the *significances*（意涵）. Fifty degrees *below zero*（零下）was to him just precisely fifty degrees below zero. It did not lead him to *meditate upon*（思索）his *frailty*（脆弱）as a *creature of temperature.*（溫度的生物）

Undoubtedly it was colder than fifty below. He *plunged in*（鑽入）among the big *spruce trees*（松樹）. Despite he was glad he was without a *sled*（雪橇）, travelling light, he was surprised at the cold. He was a warm—*whiskered*（落腮鬍）man, but the hair on his face did not protect the high cheek—bones and the eager nose that *thrust*（突出）itself aggressively into the frosty air.

At the man's heels *trotted*（輕快跑著）a dog, a big native *husky*（哈士奇）, gray—coated and without difference from its brother, the wild wolf. The animal's *instinct*（本能）knew that it was no time for travelling. In reality, it was not merely colder than fifty below zero; it was colder than sixty below, than seventy below. It was seventy—five below zero. The dog did not know anything about thermometers. The dog had learned it wanted fire, or else to *burrow*（挖洞穴）under the snow and *cuddle*（蜷伏）its warmth away from the air.

Usually the snow *above the pools*（池水面上）had a *candied appearance*（坦誠外表）but *advertised*（告誡）the danger. At a place where the snow seemed to appear *solidity*（表面堅固）, the man *broke through*（踏破掉落）. He was angry, and *cursed*（咒罵）his luck aloud. He would have to build a fire and dry out his *foot—gear*（鞋；襪）. The *flame*（火苗）he got by touching a *match*（火柴）to *a small shred of birch—bark*（一小片撕碎的樺樹皮）that he took from his pocket. Placing it on the *foundation*（火堆）, he fed the young flame with dry grass and with the tiniest dry *twigs*（樹枝）.

He worked slowly and carefully, *keenly aware of*（敏銳知道）his danger. Gradually, as the flame grew stronger, he increased the size of the twigs with which he fed it. He knew there must be no failure. When it is seventy—five below zero, a man must not fail in his first attempt to build a fire—that is, if his feet are wet.

But he was safe, for the fire was beginning to burn with strength. He was feeding it with twigs the size of his finger. But it was his own fault or his mistake. He *should not have built the fire under the spruce tree*. He should have built it in the open. Now the tree carried an *overweight*（過重）of snow on its *boughs*（樹枝）. One bough, high up in the tree, *capsized its load of snow*（傾洩下樹幹的積雪）. It grew like an *avalanche*（雪崩）, *descended upon*（掉落在）the man and the fire, and the fire was *blotted out*（撲滅）!

The man was shocked. It was as though he had just heard his own sentence of death. He made a new foundation for a fire, this time in the open. He gathered dry grasses and tiny twigs. As it flamed he held it with his teeth to the birch—bark. He *cherished*（小心；珍惜）the flame carefully and *awkwardly*（慌張地；笨拙地）. It meant life, and it must not *perish*（滅熄）. He tried to *poke*（撥火）it out with his fingers, but each twig *gushed a puff of smoke*（噴出一股煙）and went out.

As his eyes chanced on the dog, sitting across the *ruins*（廢墟）of the fire from him, the sight of the dog put a wild idea into his head. He remembered the tale of the man, who killed a *deer*（鹿）and *crawled*（爬進）inside the *carcass*（屍體）, and so was saved. He would kill the dog and bury his hands in the warm body until the *numbness*（沒有知覺）went out of them. Then he could build another fire. He got on his hands and knees and crawled toward the dog. This unusual *posture*（姿勢）again *excited suspicion*（起疑）, and the animal *sidled away*（悄悄的走開）.

The man sat up in the snow for a moment and struggled for calmness. He realized that he could not kill the dog. There was no way to do it. With his helpless hands he could neither draw nor hold his knife.

A certain fear of death came to him. This threw him into a *panic*（恐慌）, and he turned and ran up the *creek—bed*（河床）along the *trail*（小徑）. The dog joined in behind and kept up with him. He ran blindly, in fear such as he had never known in his life. And yet, when he touched his nose or cheeks, there was no *sensation*

（感覺）. Running would not *thaw them out*（融化）. Nor would it thaw out his hands and feet. This time the shivering came more quickly upon the man. He was losing in his battle with the frost. It was *creeping into*（漫延）his body from all sides. It was his last panic.

He sat up and *entertained*（懷抱）in his mind the conception（想法）of meeting death with *dignity*（尊嚴）. A good idea, he thought, to sleep off to death. It was like taking an *anesthetic*（麻醉劑）. Freezing was not so bad as people thought. There were lots worse ways to die.

Then the man *drowsed off*（迷糊中睡去）into what seemed to him the most comfortable and satisfying sleep he had ever known. But the man remained silent. Later, the dog *whined*（鼻子哼出的聲音）loudly. And still later it crept close to the man and caught the *scent of death*（死亡的氣息）. This made the animal *bristle*（毛豎立）and back away. Then it turned and trotted up the trail in the direction of the camp it knew, where were the other food-providers and fire-providers.

四、作品延伸作業

所謂「人心惟危」，「求生」成了小說中，一個極佳發掘人性的索引題材。以傑克倫敦社會主義的思想，北國、旅人與狼犬的背景、人物與野獸組合，他的象徵與隱含的意思為何？

史蒂芬‧克蘭《海上扁舟》
——怒海中的人性光輝

史蒂芬‧克蘭
(Stephen Crane, 1871 –1900)

✒ **小說特徵**
自然主義與印象派的結合

Stephen Crane's fiction presents a "symbiosis" of Naturalistic ideals and Impressionistic methods. A story, truth to life itself was the only test, and simple is truth.

-Sergio Perosa

史蒂芬克蘭小說呈現是一自然主義理想與印象派方法的合成。小說惟一標準就是生活的真實感,而簡單就是真實。

——塞吉歐培洛沙

一、作者短評

史蒂芬克蘭（Stephen Crane），1871年，出生於美國新澤西州，自幼多病，父親是衛理公會（Methodist）牧師，史蒂芬克蘭四歲即能提筆寫作，先就讀Claverack軍校，雖未久離校這段時光卻為他日後勝任戰地記者與創作戰爭小說上，提供了極大幫助。

史蒂芬克蘭，之後，在拉法葉學院（Lafayette College）及雪城大學（Syracuse University）各讀了一年書，進入報社工作。1892年，因報導有關工人罷工事件，遭報社解顧。1893年，史蒂芬克蘭在紐約只好擔任自由記者（free lancer）討生活，他深入貧民窟採訪，寫成了他的第一本小說《梅姬：一個阻街女郎》，講述了女主角梅姬因被愛人所陷，成為妓女的悲慘境遇，被讚譽是美國有關貧民窟最寫實小說。1894年發表小說《紅色英勇勳章》（The Red Badge of Courage.），以美國內戰為內容，描述戰場心理與恐怖，逼真有如親臨現場，樹立了他在美國文壇上不可動搖的地位。

1896年，史蒂芬克蘭因幫兩名妓女作偽證，官司鬧得揚揚沸沸，全國矚目下，使他聲名大損，此時美國擴張主義正盛，極欲吞併古巴，與西班牙關係已到一觸即發的戰爭邊緣，趁此，史蒂芬克蘭接受報社的邀約，改換跑道，當上了戰地記者，首件差使，正是前往古巴採訪，在佛羅里達州的Jacksonville等船期間，也結識日後不離不棄31歲的柯拉泰勒（Cora Taylor），這也是他人生最後一件幸運之事，不久，等到搭上SS Commodore汽船出海，大霧中觸礁，棄船逃生，在海上漂流30小時後，終於上岸得救。史蒂芬克蘭就是根據這次經歷，寫成短篇小說《海上扁舟》（The Open Boat），細緻地描寫了四人如何在茫茫大海中掙扎與求生的過程，是美國最著名短篇小說之一。

1898年，美、西為爭奪古巴開戰，克蘭再次去古巴採訪美西戰爭。由於史蒂芬克蘭自《紅色英勇勳章》後，接續作品銷路不佳，克蘭在美國文壇咸認是江郎才盡之下，與柯拉移居英國發展寫作生涯，依不見起色，加上健康與財務困擾不斷，1900年，肺病過逝，年僅28歲。

二、作品分析

相較畢爾斯以戰爭及傑克倫敦以自然為背景的寫實題材，史蒂芬克蘭兩者兼具，三人可說是最具美國自然主義特色及代表的小說家。克蘭的《紅色英勇勳章》、《梅姬：一個阻街女郎》與所選短篇小說《海上扁舟》，主角不論是在貧民窟、戰場與大海環境，都採取自然主義作品方式，將主角個人獨立於社會、上帝及自然之上，身陷在生與死、理想與現實及勇氣與怯懦的對立之間，沒有浪漫的樂觀主義，只有人性的堅韌與脆弱，簡單呈現人心惟危時的赤裸寫實，這在他《梅姬：一個阻街女郎》寫道：

「這本書表明，環境在這個世界上舉足輕重，它往往毫不留情地塑造人們的生活。」。

　　惟史蒂芬克蘭描寫一個人對恐懼的感情反應時，似乎更多了一份強調在人性恐懼時，那一絲可貴的人性光輝展現，《海上扁舟》中，四人海上漂流時，面對一再遭遇的失望與無助，都是充滿扶持互助感情。

　　史蒂芬克蘭作品除具備自然與寫實的特徵外，另外就是他習慣在小說中，對景色的光線與明暗的描寫，就像是印象主義畫家一般，他以文學小說中充滿生動活潑的色彩及形象而聞名，在《海上扁舟》中，一開頭：

　　「已沒有人知道天空的顏色。他們的眼光都平坦鎖定不斷向他們襲來的海浪，除了浪端的泡沫白色，海浪已像是調色盤一般，他們對大海的顏色已是瞭如指掌。」，克蘭習慣性描繪光景的內容，隨處可見。

三、閱讀文選

The Open Boat

Stephen Crane

These waves were *abrupt*（險惡）and tall, and each *froth—top*（浪端泡沫）was a problem in small—boat *navigation*（航行）. As the *crest of each wave*（浪頭）was a *hill*（小山）, her *stern*（船尾）*plopped down*（噗通掉下）and the *spray splashed*（海花四濺）past them. The wind *tore through*（撕開著）the hair of the four hatless men.

"It's an *on—shore wind*（上岸的風）," said the cook.

"That's right," said the *correspondent*（記者）.

The busy *oiler nodded.*（油料工點頭同意）

"Oh, well," said the captain, *soothing*（安撫）his children, "We'll *get ashore all right*（安全上岸）."

In the meantime the oiler and the correspondent *rowed*（划船）. And also they rowed.

"See it?" said the captain.

"No," said the correspondent slowly, "I didn't see anything."

"Look again," said the captain. He pointed. "It's exactly in that direction."

At the top of another wave, and this time his eyes *chanced on*（不經意）a small *still*（靜止的）thing on the edge of the horizon.

It was a *light house*（燈塔）so tiny.

"Think *we'll make it*（我們可以活著逃出）, captain? If this wind holds and the boat don't *swamp*（浸水）."

"*Bail her*（舀水出船）, cook," said the captain *serenely*（沉著地）.

"All right, captain," said the cheerful cook.

It would be difficult to describe the *subtle brotherhood*（微妙的手足之情）of men that was here established on the seas. They were a captain, an oiler, a cook, and a correspondent, and they were friends, friends in a more curiously *iron—bound degree*（如鐵凝固般）than may be common.

Meanwhile the lighthouse had been growing slowly larger. It had now almost *assumed color*（呈現顏色）, and appeared like a little grey shadow on the sky.

"Take her easy, now, boys," said the captain. "Don't spend yourselves. You'll need all your strength, because we'll sure have to swim for it. Take your time."

Slowly the land arose from the sea.

"That's the *house of refuge*（避難屋）, sure," said the cook. "They'll see us *before long*（很快地）, and come out after us."

… the little boat turned her nose once more *down the wind*（順風）, and all but the *oarsman*（滑槳人）watched the shore grow. In an hour, perhaps, they would be ashore.

"Cook," remarked the captain, "there don't seem to be any signs of life about your house of refuge."

"No," replied the cook. "Funny they don't see us!"

The lightheartedness of a former time had completely faded.

"Well," said the captain, *ultimately*（最後）, "I suppose we'll have to make a try for ourselves. If we stay out here too long, we'll none of us have strength left to swim after the boat swamps."

And so the oiler, who was at the oars, turned the boat straight for the shore. The *billows*（大浪）that came at this time were more *formidable*（巨大的）. There was a *considerable*（相當的）silence as the boat *bumped over the sea to deeper water*（在大海上上下顛簸）.

"What do you think of those life—saving people? "

"Funny they haven't seen us."

"Maybe they think we're out here for sport! Maybe they think we're fishing. Maybe they think we're damned fools."

"Look! There's a man on the shore!"

"Where?"

"There! See 'im? See 'im?"

"Now he's stopped. Look! He's facing us!"

"What's he doing now?"

"Is he waving at us?"

"No, not now! he was, though."

"Look! There comes another man!"

"That's it, likely. Look! There's a fellow waving a little black flag. "

"That ain't a flag, is it? That's his coat. Why, certainly, that's his coat."

"What's that idiot with the coat mean? What's he signaling, anyhow?"

"It looks as if he were trying to tell us to go north. There must be a life—saving station up there."

"No! He thinks we're fishing."

"Well, I wish I could make something out of those signals. What do you suppose he means?"

"He not mean anything. He's just playing."

The shore grew *dusky*（黑暗）. This was surely a quiet evening. The cook looked without interest at the water. Finally he spoke. "Billie," he *murmured*（喃喃自語）, "what kind of pie do you like best?"

"Pie," said the oiler and the correspondent, *agitatedly*（騷動地）. Don't talk about those things, *blast you !*（dame you!婉轉語）"

"Well," said the cook, "I was just thinking about ham sandwiches, and—"

The captain, in the *bow*（船首）, "Pretty long night," he observed to the correspondent. He looked at the shore.

"Did you see that *shark*（鯊魚）playing around?"

"Yes, I saw him. He was a big fellow, all right."

"Wish I had known you were awake."

When the correspondent again opened his eyes, the *monstrous in—shore rollers*（近岸捲曲大浪）*heaved*（上下波動）the boat high until the men saw the *slanted*（歪斜般的）beach. "We won't get in very close," said the captain. "Now, boys," said the captain, "she is going to swamp, sure. All we can do is to work her in as far as possible, and then when she swamps, pile out and *scramble for the beach*（拼命搶上沙灘）. Keep cool now, and don't jump until she swamps sure."

But the next crest crashed also. The tumbling, boiling flood of white water caught the boat and whirled it. Water swarmed in from all sides....

The little boat, *drunken with this weight of water*（吃了與船一樣的水重）, *reeled*（捲入）deeper into the sea.

"Bail her out, cook! Bail her out," said the captain.

"All right, captain," said the cook.

"Now, boys, the next one will do for us, sure," said the oiler. "Mind to jump *clear of*（離開；保持距離）the boat."

The third wave moved forward, huge, *furious*（猛烈的）, *implacable*（無情的）. It fairly swallowed the *dingy*（小舟）, and almost simultaneously the men *tumbled i*nto（摔下）the sea.

"Come to the boat," called the captain.

"All right, captain." As the correspondent *paddled*（划水）, each wave *knocked him into a heap*（打進水堆）, and the *under—tow*（水下的拖引）pulled at him.

Then he saw the man had been running and bounding into the water. He *dragged ashore*（拖⋯上岸）the cook, and then *waded towards*（跋涉向）the captain, but the captain waved him away, and sent him to the correspondent. He gave a strong pull, and a long drag at the correspondent's hand.

In the shallows, face downward, lay the oiler. His forehead touched sand that was between each wave.

It seems that instantly the beach was populated with men with *blankets*（毛毯）, clothes, and women with coffeepots and all the *remedies*（醫藥）. The welcome of the land to the men from the sea was warm and *generous*（慷慨）, but *a still and dripping shape*（不動、正著滴水的人形——暗指油料工屍體）was carried slowly up the beach.

When it came night, the white waves paced to and fro in the moonlight, and the wind brought the sound of the great sea's voice to the men on shore, and they felt that they could then be interpreters.

四、作品延伸作業

　　相較傑克倫敦《生火》，描繪求生讓人生失去了人性，必需有如野獸般的生存，史蒂芬克蘭的《海上扁舟》在寫作的氛圍與目的，你以為有何分別？

10 海明威《白象似的群山》
——無聲勝有聲的弦外之音

小說特徵

「冰山理論」
（The Theory of Iceberg）

歐內斯特・海明威
（Ernest Hemingway, 1899 –1961）

I always try to write on the principal of the iceberg. Anything you know you can eliminate and it only strengthens your iceberg. It is the part that doesn't show.

-Ernest Hemingway

我總試著以「冰山原則」寫作。凡是已知的，盡皆刪去；只要強固你冰山下隱藏的那一部分。

——海明威

一、作者短評

如果要挑選一位最能展現美國民族性格——粗獷、浪漫、坦率、直接，不說廢話的小說家代表，給我海明威，其餘免談！

海明威（Ernest Miller Hemingway），1899年，出生於美國伊利諾的芝加哥市，身型魁梧偉岸，充滿男人陽剛形象。海明威一生以戰爭、美人、醇酒為尚，與鬥牛、釣魚、狩獵為伍，風流浪漫中，感情錯綜複雜，先後結過四次婚，是一次大戰後，美國「失落的一代」（the lost generation）狂歡、頹廢與迷茫、徬徨形象鮮明的代表，他豪邁與大膽的男性意識，無遺的表現在他作品之中，使戰爭與性愛成為他文學的兩大主題特色。

海明威視戰場為浪漫與英雄主義的聖地，每次爆發戰爭，他都不顧生死的奔赴戰場，《戰地春夢》即是他刻劃一次大戰所造成人類無可彌補的創傷，《戰地鐘聲》則以西班牙內戰為背景，二次大戰，海明威照樣不落人後，堪稱是最Man的小說家。一九五四年《老人與海》，為他贏得了諾貝爾文學獎。海明威創作《老人與海》時，把一切不必要向讀者交代的內容都統統刪除，只突出人物和故事情節，因此，他把社會背景淡化了，而更加側重於人物的內心獨白和動作，其他人物，都是淡淡幾筆勾勒其模糊的形象，給人朦朦朧朧的感覺。

海明威除在戰爭的暴力中，尋找英雄浪漫，激勵人道精神外，性愛與性別是他另一個極其曖昧的小說主題；文中常現柔順甜美、面目模糊的弱勢女子，如男性的附屬，這在《白象似的群山》中男主角希望女主角墮胎或《戰地春夢》中女主角凱薩琳勇於當未婚媽媽，最後難產、母子皆死的結局，似乎也是反射海明威沉湎於性愛歡樂，不願當父親的性格寫照。

　　海明威的寫作風格以簡潔著稱，對美國文學及20世紀文學的發展有極深遠的影響；最足具體代表者，莫過他所提出「冰山原則」已是小說創作與欣賞之圭臬，簡白式的文體吸引了大批仿效者，掀起了小說寫作上的臨摹風潮，固然，這與他記者出身，要簡不繁的文筆訓練大有關係，但文如其人，更是他愛恨分明，感情直接的性格寫照。

　　1961年7月2日，海明威久病厭世，在家中以獵槍自殺身亡。

二、作品分析

　　海明威提出小說之「冰山理論」（The Theory of Iceberg），就是以最簡約的對白，看似冰山在水面上的小露，其實隱含了水面下的暗潮洶湧，也是這股「無聲勝有聲，弦外之音」的奧妙，反令人屏息以待。海明威的小說《白象似的群山》公認是此一「冰山理論」典範之作，文中男女主角沒有確切的身份，沒有外貌，故事也沒有歷史時間，可是讀者不會感到話題的陌生，也沒有消化閱讀的困難。一開場，女人以一座如白象的山脈，撩起話題，男人則心不在焉，一心一意只想說服女孩墮胎。兩人攻防之間衝突，自此，一直都是有形無形地的存在著；許多次一來一往間，言不及義的對話，像各自佈局的心理戰。我們當然明白，表面上佔上風的看來是女子，但是私下操縱全局的仍是他的男人。男人策略總是以一切「為她著想」
的哄騙，讓女人甘心接受「手術」（是全文最接近墮胎的字
眼），對話中，男人威逼利誘、不負責任的逃避心態表現無
遺，女子無奈、鬱悶及絕望，終於在憤怒中爆發，吶喊著：
"Would you please please please please please please please stop talking."
中宣洩殆盡時，轉念之間，女子最後也只能屈服男人的陽剛，
悲愴以："There's nothing wrong with me. I feel fine." 話下結局，
強顏歡笑將眼前的苦酒與悲傷，一飲而盡，道盡女人在男人、
墮胎兩難間的委曲求全，令人為女子的犧牲與卑微更加不捨，
全篇欲蓋彌彰，張力十足的交鋒對話，讓你不得不佩服海明威
簡單有力的心靈震撼！

三、閱讀文選

Hills Like White Elephants

Ernest Hemingway

The *hills*（山脈）across the *valley*（山谷）of the Ebro were
long and white. *Close against*（緊靠）the station there was a bar
with a *curtain*（窗簾）, made of *strings of bamboo beads*（竹作的
串珠）, *hung across*（橫掛在）the open door into the bar, to keep
out flies. The American and the girl with him sat at a table in the
shade（遮蔭處）, outside the bar. It was very hot and the *express*

（特快車）from Barcelona would come in forty minutes. It stopped at this *junction*（交會站）for two minutes and went on to *Madrid*（馬德里）. The girl was looking off at the line of hills. They were white in the sun and the country was brown and dry.

I

"They look like white elephants," she said.

"I've never seen one," the man drank his beer.

"No, you wouldn't have."

"I might have, just because you say I wouldn't have doesn't prove anything（意指：不是妳說了就算）," the man said.

II

The girl looked at the bead curtain.

"They've painted something on it," she said.

" What does it say?"

"Anis del Toro. It's a drink." "Could we try it? "

The man called "Listen" through the curtain. The woman came out from the bar.

"We want two Anis del Toro."

"With water? "

"Do you want it with water?"

"I don't know," the girl said. "Is it good with water?"

"You want them with water?" asked the woman.

"Yes, with water."

"It tastes like *licorice*（甘草）," the girl said.

"That's the way with everything."

"Yes," said the girl. "Everything tastes of licorice. Especially all the things you've waited so long for, like *absinthe*（苦艾酒）."

"Oh, *cut it out.*" （別再說了！）

"You started it," the girl said.

"I was being *amused.*（好玩有趣的）Well, let's try and have a fine time."

"All right. I was trying. I said the mountains looked like white elephants. Wasn't that bright?"

"That was bright. I wanted to try this new drink. That's all we do, isn't it—look at things and try new drinks?"

"I guess so." The girl looked across at the hills. "They're lovely hills," she said.

III

The warm wind blew the bead curtain against the table.

"The beer's nice and cool," the man said.

"It's lovely," the girl said.

"It's really a simple *operation*（手術）, Jig," the man said.

"It's not really an operation at all. " The girl looked at the ground.

"I know you wouldn't mind it, Jig. It's really not anything. It's just to let the air in. "

The girl did not say anything.

"I'll go with you and I'll stay with you all the time. They just let the air in and then it's all perfectly natural."

"Then what will we do afterward?" the girl said.

"We'll be fine afterward. Just like we were before."

The girl looked at the bead curtain, put her hand out and took hold of two of the strings of beads.

" And you think then we'll be all right and be happy."

"I know we will. You don't have to be afraid. I've known lots of people that have done it."

"So have I," said the girl. "And afterward they were all so happy."

"Well," the man said, "if you don't want to you don't have to. I wouldn't have you do it if you didn't want to. But I know it's perfectly simple."

"And if I do it you'll be happy and things will be like they were and you'll love me?"

"I love you now. You know I love you.", the man said,

"If I do it you won't ever worry?"

"I won't worry about that because it's perfectly simple."

"Then I'll do it. Because I don't care about me."

"What do you mean?" "I don't care about me."

"Well, I care about you. And I'll do it and then everything will be fine."

"I don't want you to do it if you feel that way."

VI

The girl stood up and walked to the end of the station. The shadow of a cloud moved across the field of *grain*（麥田）and trees along the banks of the Ebro.

"And we could have all this," she said.

"What did you say?"

"I said we could have everything."

"No, we can't."

"We can have the whole world."

"No, we can't."

"We can go everywhere."

"No, we can't. It isn't ours any more."

"It's ours."

"No, it isn't. And once they take it away, you never get it back."

They sat down at the table and the girl looked across at the hills on the dry side of the valley.

"You've got to realize," he said, "that I don't want you to do it if you don't want to. "

"Doesn't it mean anything to you? "

"Of course it does. I don't want any one else. And I know it's perfectly simple."

"Yes, you know it's perfectly simple."

"It's all right for you to say that, but I do know it."

"Would you do something for me now? "

" I'd do anything for you.'

" Would you please please please please please please please Stop talking. "

"But I don't want you to," he said,

"I don't care anything about it." "I'll scream," the girl said.

V

The woman came out through the curtains with two glasses of beer. "The train comes in five minutes," she said. The girl smiled brightly at the woman, to thank her.

"I'd better take the bags over to the other side of the station," the man said. " All right. Then come back and we'll finish the beer." She was sitting at the table and smiled at him.

"Do you feel better?" he asked.

"I feel fine," she said. "There's nothing wrong with me. I feel fine."

四、作品延伸作業

　　海明威《白象似的群山》，人物簡單，角色上只有Bar Woman 和男、女主角三人，全文有如劇本，都以對白呈現，男人哄騙利誘的逃避心態與女子委曲壓抑的心理，劇力十足。嘗試以四人一組（一人任旁白）的話劇方式演出。

歐・亨利《最後一片葉子》
——短篇小說驚奇之王

歐・亨利
(O. Henry, 1862 –1910)

小說特徵

「歐・亨利式急轉彎」
（O. Henry's twist）

"......and—look out the window at the last ivy leaf on the wall. Didn't you wonder why it never fluttered or moved when the wind blew? Ah, darling, it's Behrman's masterpiece—he painted it there the night that the last leaf fell."

-O. Henry , The Last Leaf

看著窗外攀爬在牆上的最後一片葉子。（蘇與喬安娜）不覺奇怪這片葉子從不隨風飄揚或移動過？啊！親愛的，它是伯曼的傑作，是那晚，當最後一片葉子落下時，他畫上的。

——歐・亨利《最後一片葉子》

一、作者短評

　　歐‧亨利（O. Henry），1862年，出身於美國北卡羅來納州一個小鎮醫師家庭，原名威廉‧西德尼‧波特（William Sydney Porter），是美國最著名的短篇小說家之一，曾被評論界譽為美國現代短篇小說之父。

　　歐‧亨利的一生富於傳奇性，當過藥房學徒、牛仔、會計員、土地辦事員、新聞記者、銀行出納員。當銀行出納員時，受疑挪用銀行現金，被捕入獄，獄中擔任醫務室的藥劑師時，開始認真寫作。獲釋後，1902年移居紐約，改名歐‧亨利，決心從事寫作專業。歐‧亨利善於描寫美國社會，尤其是紐約百姓的生活，歐‧亨利有很多的小說以紐約為背景，他筆下的紐約是個怪事層出不窮的大都市。

　　歐‧亨利寫小說一心目的者乃「供讀者消遣」，他的作品構思新穎，幽默的語言始終貫穿，但結局絕對出人意外，讓人跌破眼鏡，這種出其不意，情節逆轉的結尾收場，所謂「歐‧亨利式急轉彎」（O. Henry's twist），成為了他小說中最大的特色。

　　代表作有小說集《白菜與國王》、《四百萬》、《命運之路》等。其中一些名篇如《愛的犧牲》、《警察與讚美詩》、《帶傢具出租的房間》、《麥琪的禮物》、《最後一片葉子》等使他獲得了世界聲譽。

二、作品分析

　　馬奎斯說過「每一篇好的小說都是這世界的一個謎。」，但決定小說的引人入勝與否，謎題的揭曉技巧，終究才是關鍵。如果你喜歡享受Surprise或跌碎眼鏡的感覺，歐・亨利的短篇小說應該是不會使你失望的選擇。這歸功於他小說中最慣用和稱道的寫作策略──「歐・亨利式急轉彎」。

　　歐・亨利在每篇作品，當他開始慢慢鋪陳劇情的時候，總是利用讀者直線的思考方式，誤導歧途，其實早有一條細微的線索或精緻的伏筆隱藏其中，以至於當故事推展至最高潮時，筆鋒一轉，倏忽之間，總是以出人意料的結尾，畫下句點，讀者錯愕瞬間，往往先是出人意料，但經仔細一想，又會覺得其實合情合理，令人格外拍案叫絕，回味無窮。歐・亨利幾乎在每一篇作品中都運用了這樣的寫作的佈局與技巧，讓讀者即使知道正面對一個說故事的「詐騙集團」，卻仍「甘心情願」期待享受被騙的驚喜。歐・亨利的小說世界如此充滿魅力，這也使得大多數人只要一談起歐・亨利的小說，立即浮現腦海的往往是某一篇故事裡的情節，而不是某一篇故事中的人物；他的「歐・亨利式結局」也成了一種文學創作模式，已是許多作家模仿的經典。

　　《最後一片葉子》是以紐約為背景，講述一群潦倒的藝術家彼此扶持的故事；畫家Johnsy生了病，失去求生意識，她看著窗外抵擋不過風雨的葉子，一片一片飄落，悲觀地倒數自己的生命。同時，樓下窮途潦倒，脾氣暴躁，吹噓要畫下一生傑作的老畫家伯曼，知道了這件事後，竟在風雨夜偷偷在牆頭畫上了一片永不掉落的葉子，鼓舞了Johnsy的求生意志，進而康復，伯曼卻因此染上急性肺炎死了。歐·亨利以人道、幽默的深情筆觸，對社會底層的小人物予以特別關注，也將痛苦與幽默及悲慘與幸福，做了奇特混合，讓他小說除驚奇之外，擁有著獨特的人文關懷。

三、閱讀文選

The Last Leaf

O. Henry

Many artists lived in the *Greenwich Village*（格林威治村；美國各類藝術家的聚居地）area of New York. Two young women named Sue and Johnsy shared a *studio*（工作室）*apartment*（公寓）at the top of a *three—story*（三層樓）building. Johnsy's real name was Joanna.

In November, a cold, unseen stranger came to visit the city. This disease, *pneumonia*（肺炎）, killed many people. Johnsy lay on her bed, hardly moving. She looked through the small window. She could see *the side of the brick housenext to her building*（隔壁磚屋的牆面）.

One morning, a doctor examined Johnsy and *took her temperature*（量體溫）. Then he spoke with Sue in another room.

"She has one chance in—let us say ten," he said. "And that chance is for her to want to live. Your friend has *made up her mind*（決心）that she is not going to get well. Has she anything on her mind?"

"She—she wanted to paint in Italy some day," said Sue.

"Paint?" said the doctor. "Bosh! Has she anything on her mind *worth*（值得）thinking twice—a man for example?"

"A man?" said Sue. "Is a man worth—but, no, doctor; there is nothing of the kind."

"I will do all that science can do," said the doctor. "But whenever my patient begins to *count the carriage sat her funeral*（計算葬禮運輸費用）, I take away fifty percent from the *curative*（治療）power of medicines."

After the doctor had gone, Sue went into the workroom and cried. Then she went to Johnsy's room with her *drawing board*（畫板）, *whistling ragtime*（哼著爵士樂）.

Johnsy lay with her face toward the window. Johnsy's eyes were open wide. She was looking out the window and *counting*（數著）—*counting backward*（倒數著）. "Twelve," she said , and a little later "eleven"; and then "ten" and "nine"; and then "eight" and "seven," almost together.

Sue looked out the window. What was there to count? An old *ivy vine*（長春藤）climbed half way up *the blank side of the house*（房子空壁上）seven meters away. The cold breath of autumn had *stricken leaves*（摧殘著葉子）from the plant hung on there.

"What is it, dear?" asked Sue.

"Six," said Johnsy, quietly. "They're falling faster now. Three days ago there were almost a hundred. There goes another one. There are only five left now."

"Five what, dear?" asked Sue.

"Leaves. On the plant. When the last one falls I must go, too. I've known that for three days. Didn't the doctor tell you?"

"Oh, I never heard of such a thing," said Sue. "What have old ivy leaves to do with your getting well? *Don't be silly*（別傻了！）. The doctor told me this morning that your chances for getting well real soon—he said the chances were ten to one! Try to eat some soup now. And, let me go back to my drawing, so I can sell it to the magazine and buy food and wine for us."

"There goes another one. No, I don't want any soup. That leaves just four. I want to see the last one fall before it gets dark. Then I'll go, too."

"Johnsy, dear," said Sue, "will you promise me to keep your eyes closed, and not look out the window until I am done working? I must hand those drawings in by tomorrow."

"I want to see the last one fall. I'm tired of waiting. I'm tired of thinking. I want to *turn loose my hold on everything*（放手一切）, and go *sailing down*（隨風而去）, just like one of those poor, tired leaves."

"Try to sleep," said Sue. "I must call Mister Behrman up to be my model for my drawing of an old *miner*（礦工）. Don't try to move until I come back."

Old Behrman was a painter who lived on the *ground floor*（一樓）of the apartment building. Behrman was a *failure*（失敗）in art. For years, he had always been planning to paint a work of art, but had never yet begun it. He earned a little money by serving as a model to artists who could not pay for a professional model. He was a *fierce*（激烈；瘋狂的）, little, old man who protected the two young women in the studio apartment above him.

Sue told him about Johnsy and how she feared that her friend would *float away*（飄落）like a leaf. Old Behrman was angered at such an idea. "Are there people in the world with the foolishness to die because leaves drop off a vine? Why do you let that *silly business*（蠢事）come in her brain?"

"She is very sick and *weak*（體弱）," said Sue, "and the disease has left her mind full of strange ideas."

"This is not any place in which one so good as Miss Johnsy shall lie sick," *yelled*（尖叫）Behrman. "Some day I will paint a *masterpiece*（傑作）, and we shall all go away."

Johnsy was sleeping when they went upstairs. Sue *pulled the shade*（拉起遮簾）down to cover the window. She and Behrman went into the other room. They looked out a window fearfully at the ivy vine. Then they looked at each other without speaking. A cold rain was falling, mixed with snow. Behrman sat and posed as the miner.

The next morning, Sue awoke after an hour's sleep. She found Johnsy with wide─open eyes staring at the covered window.

"Pull up the shade; I want to see," she ordered, quietly.

Sue obeyed.

After the beating rain and fierce wind that blew through the night, there yet stood against the wall one ivy leaf. It was the last one on the vine. It was still dark green at the center. But its *edges*（葉緣）were colored with the yellow. It hung *bravely*（勇敢地）from the branch about seven meters above the ground.

"It is the last one," said Johnsy. "I thought it would surely fall during the night. I heard the wind. It will fall today and I shall die at the same time."

"Dear, dear!" said Sue, *leaning*（倚靠）her *worn face*（憔悴面容）down toward the bed. "Think of me, if you won't think of yourself. What would I do?"

But Johnsy did not answer.

The next morning, when it was light, Johnsy demanded that the window shade be raised. The ivy leaf was still there. Johnsy lay for a long time, looking at it. And then she called to Sue, who was preparing chicken soup.

"I've been a bad girl," said Johnsy. "Something has made that last leaf stay there to show me how bad I was. It is wrong to want to die. You may bring me a little soup now."

An hour later she said: "Someday I hope to paint the Bay of Naples."

Later in the day, the doctor came, and Sue talked to him in the hallway.

"*Even chances*（機會一半一半了！）," said the doctor. "With good care, you'll win. And now I must see another case I have in your building. Behrman, his name is—some kind of an artist, I believe. Pneumonia, too. He is an old, weak man and his case is severe. There is no hope for him; but he goes to the hospital today to ease his pain."

The next day, the doctor said to Sue: "She's out of danger. You won. *nutrition*（營養）and care now—that's all."

Later that day, Sue came to the bed where Johnsy lay, and put one arm around her.

"I have something to tell you," she said. "Mister Behrman died of pneumonia today in the hospital. He was sick only two days. When they found him the morning in his room , his shoes and clothing were completely wet and icy cold. They could not imagine where he had been on such a terrible night. And then they found a lantern（燈）, still lighted. And they found a *ladder*（梯子）that had been moved from its place. And a *painting board*（調色盤）with green and yellow colors mixed on it.

And look out the window, dear, at the last ivy leaf on the wall. Didn't you wonder why it never moved when the wind blew? Ah, darling, it is Behrman's masterpiece—he painted it there the night that the last leaf fell."

四、作品延伸作業

「歐・亨利式急轉彎」，已是現在幽默如笑話急轉彎的常態應用。

「最後一片葉子」故事最後結局：蘇西在好友安娜的細心照顧下日漸康復，但老畫家卻因在暴風雨中畫上最後一片葉子而一病不起，最後過世，以悲傷做故事的結尾。

假如你是作者，你以喜劇式的twist，會怎麼編排故事的結局呢？讓我們試著改編一下吧！

12 王爾德《自私的巨人》
——淒美動人的快樂王子

小說特徵

悲劇性唯美主義
（aestheticism）

奧斯卡·王爾德
（Oscar Wilde, 1854 –1900）

We are all in the gutter, but some of us are looking at the stars.

-Oscar Wilde

我們都生活在陰溝裏，但仍有人仰望星空。

——奧斯卡·王爾德

一、作者短評

　　奧斯卡‧王爾德（Oscar Wilde, 1854~1900），愛爾蘭作家、詩人、戲劇家，英國唯美主義（aestheticism）倡導者。王爾德天生才氣縱橫、魅力十足，學術信念上以追求希臘美學為宗；生活上也身體力行這樣的理念，講究打扮，喜好華服的他，在當時保守的社會風氣中，雖顯得「奇裝異服、特立獨行」，王爾德卻依然故我，一如他力求藝術創作的唯美堅持。

　　王爾德有如他作品「快樂王子」，充滿著敏感與悲劇命運特質，吸引著每一個人的目光，但同時，他特立獨行，不受世俗規範，招來社會眾人的側目；加上他「同志」身份，一旦勇於「出櫃」，在嚴守禮教的的英國維多利亞時代，注定為他帶來災難。一八九五年一場同性戀控告案，將王爾德如日中天的聲譽事業毀於一旦，被判入獄的同時，王爾德宣告破產，出獄後流亡法國，抑鬱而終。

　　十九世紀，王爾德和蕭伯納並列當時英國的才子，王爾德作品中所呈現悲劇性的美，為他的文創帶來極大的渲染力，足以深深地撼動人心；但真正為王爾德贏得名譽的是他的童話作品，王爾德寫給他的好友 G. Kerstey 信裡提到：「我的童話，部分是為了孩子，部分是為了那些還擁有童心的成人們。」他所寫的童話，故事結構總是呈現了淡淡的哀傷，淒美優雅，不落俗套，卻又夾帶著幽默、戲謔的華麗文筆，抨擊社會上保守、迂腐的風氣，引起當時社會大眾的共鳴和爭議，也因為其所帶來的衝擊性，也是與一般傳統童話藝術價值不同的地方。

二、作品分析

王爾德作品與其稱之唯美主義，不如以淒美主義更近真實。王爾德生平除了劇作和小說之外，創作出九篇令人驚豔的童話故事，在1888年創作的《快樂王子及其他故事》（The Happy Prince and Other Tales）中的三篇經典故事——〈快樂王子〉裡，王子與燕子為了幫助貧苦人民，而犧牲自己；〈夜鶯與玫瑰〉中，夜鶯為了學生想要一朵紅玫瑰，結果以身體的血染紅了花瓣，綻放出美麗的紅玫瑰花朵；在〈自私的巨人〉裡，原本討厭小孩子的巨人，最終還是感受到孩童的純真，並體認到「我有許多美麗的花朵，但是孩子們才是最美的」。雖然這三則故事的結局，都存在著死亡的陰影，但感不到絲毫之可怕，反是感動，王爾德的作品，始終展現出人性中至善至美的光輝層面。

在王爾德的童話中，《自私的巨人》是篇幅最短的一篇，也最富有優美、詩意的一篇。一次，王爾德給兒子講《自私的巨人》，竟然情不自禁哭了起來。兒子問他為什麼哭了，王爾德說，真正美麗的事物總會使他流下眼淚。這也是何以王爾德的故事中，往往沒有王子與公主的完美結尾的戀愛，也沒有皆大歡喜的結局，但因為它貼近人性的一面，淒美比完美更動人，沒有happy ending的童話故事，反更有其好看之處！

三、閱讀文選

The Selfish Giant

Oscar Wilde

Every afternoon, as they were coming from school, the children *used to*（曾經）go and play in the Giant's garden.

It was a large lovely garden, with soft green grass. Here and there over the grass stood beautiful flowers like stars. The birds sat on the trees and sang so sweetly. "How happy we are here!" they cried to each other.

One day the Giant came back. He had been to visit his friend the Cornish *ogre*（怪物：像史瑞克）, and had stayed with him for seven years. But now he *determined to*（決定）return to his own *castle*（城堡）. When he arrived he saw the children playing in the garden.

"What are you doing here?" he cried in a very *gruff*（粗暴）voice, and the children ran away.

"My own garden is my own garden," said the Giant.

" I will allow nobody to play in it but myself." So he built a high wall all round it, and put up a *notice—board.*（告示板）

TRESPASSERS（闖入）
WILL BE PROSECUTED（必罰）

He was a very selfish Giant.

The poor children had now nowhere to play. "How happy we were there," they said to each other. Though the Spring came, the birds did not care to sing in it as there were no children, and the trees forgot to *blossom*（指果樹之花）. Flower was dressed in *grey*（灰暗）, and his breath was like ice.

"I cannot understand why the Spring is so late in coming," said the Selfish Giant, as he sat at the window and looked out at his cold white garden; "I hope there will be a change in the weather."

One morning the Giant was lying awake in bed when he heard some lovely music. It sounded so sweet that it seemed to him to be the most beautiful music in the world. "I believe the Spring has come at last," said the Giant; and he jumped out of bed and looked out.

What did he see?

He saw a most wonderful sight. Through a little *hole*（洞）in the wall the children had *crept in*（爬進）, and they were sitting in the branches of the trees. And the trees were so glad to have the children back again that they had covered themselves with blossoms. The birds were flying about and *twittering*（鳥吱吱喳喳）with delight, and the flowers were looking up through the green grass and laughing.

And the Giant's heart *melted*（融化）as he looked out. "How selfish I have been!" he said. So he crept downstairs and opened the *front door*（前門）quite softly, and went out into the garden. But when the children saw him they were so *frightened*（害怕）that they all ran away, and the garden became winter again. Only the little boy did not run, for he did not see the Giant coming. And the tree broke at once into blossom, and the birds came and sang on it, and the little boy *stretched out*（伸出）his two arms and *flung them round*（環繞）the Giant's neck, and kissed him. And the other children, when they saw that the Giant was not wicked any longer, came running back, and with them came the Spring. "It is your garden now, little children," said the Giant, and he took a great *axe*（斧頭）and knocked down the wall.

Every afternoon, when school was over, the children came and played with the Giant. But the little boy whom the Giant loved was never seen again. The Giant was very kind to all the children, yet he *longed for*（期待）his first little friend, and often spoke of him. "How I would like to see him!" he used to say.

Years went over, and the Giant grew very old and *feeble*（虛弱）. One winter morning he looked out of his window as he was dressing. It certainly was a *marvelous sight*（驚奇難信的景象）. In the farthest corner of the garden, stood the little boy he had loved.

Downstairs ran the Giant in great joy, and out into the garden. And when he came quite close his face grew red with anger, and he said, "Who hath dared to wound thee?" For on the *palms*（手掌）of the child's hands were the prints of two *nails*（釘子）, and the *prints*（印痕）of two nails were on the little feet.

"Who have dared to *wound*（傷害）you?" cried the Giant; "tell me, that I may take my big *sword*（劍）and *slay*（殺掉）him."

"Nay!" answered the child; "but these are the wounds of Love."

"Who are you?" said the Giant, and a strange *awe*（畏懼）fell on him, and he *knelt*（跪地）before the little child.

And the child smiled on the Giant, and said to him, "You let me play once in your garden, today you shall come with me to my garden, which is *Paradise*（天堂）."

And when the children ran in that afternoon, they found the Giant lying dead under the tree, all covered with white blossoms.

四、作品延伸作業

在少子化的今天，王爾德《自私的巨人》應該是最值得推廣的短篇小說，小孩的存在無異是一切快樂的必要條件，另外由巨人從自私到開放的態度，也說明了什麼樣的人生道理？

13 法蘭克・史塔頓《美女還是老虎？》
——小說的創作法寶「兩難」

小說特徵
兒童文學、童話

法蘭克・史塔頓
(Frank R. Stockton, 1834 –1902)

"It is not for me to presume to set myself up as the one person able to answer. And so I leave it with all of you."

-Frank R. Stockton

（在故事裏），我不會把自己設定為唯一能回答問題之人，所以我把答案留給各位。

——法蘭克・史塔頓

一、作者短評

　　法蘭克史塔頓（Frank R. Stockton），1834年，出生於美國費城，由於擔任牧師的父親堅決反對史塔頓走入作家行業，史塔頓只好改以木工維生，直到父親過世，史塔頓方才進入報社，專事於寫作，作品以幽默文風見長，但建立他文學地位則是他一系列之兒童文學作品，由於不流於同俗，廣受歡迎。

　　十九世紀下半年，美國大眾通俗文學蓬勃如雨後春筍，像是馬克吐溫的西部鄉土性幽默，歐亨利取材都市小人物生活故事，並以出人意外的結局取勝，同期的史塔頓則在美國文學較希罕的童話作品這一塊，兼具兩人的特色，用幽默、機智的筆觸，極力避免道德說教，在生動與幾近事實的方式下，敘述他精彩的冒險故事，挑露人性的貪心、暴力、濫權等缺憾面。他成名之作正是家喻戶曉1882年出版之《美女還是老虎？》，由於內容簡單，主題明確，史塔頓刻意保留故事結局，且反把這一任務交給了讀者，《美女還是老虎？》也成了全美甚至世界文學課堂中，最喜採用小說討論的教材。

二、作品分析

　　小說基本就是三個要素的組合——「人物」（character）與「情節」（plot），用來表現「主題」（theme）的創作。一個有戲劇張力，能吸引讀者眼光看下去的小說，固常是「（人物）性格──（主題）命運」的邏輯鋪陳，但情節的設計，卻是吸引度或深刻的關鍵，以下有幾個小說情節的創作法寶──矛盾、兩難或荒謬，通常是擴大小說生動與感染讀者的有效途徑。

「矛盾」是內在性格與外在認定的反差。譬如：霍桑在《紅字》中，設計正直虔誠的牧師與有夫之婦發生愛情，情節掙扎於道德教義與人性愛慾的矛盾之間；另外，國內九把刀的《殺手歐陽盆栽》也是殺手卻不殺人，反而救人，使劇情變得有吸引力。

「荒謬」則是時空價值的變遷，所引起的荒謬感，譬如黃春明的《蘋果的滋味》，當窮人被美國人開車撞傷，獲得應得賠償後，卻是滿懷感恩與幸運的荒謬，最能勾起昨是今非的諷刺與會心一笑。

至於，「兩難」則是個人對外部的抉擇，效果的好壞程度，則在於抉擇「是非」標準之距離，如果越近─也就是當每個答案都是答案，等於沒有答案時，則越具吸引。例如黃春明的《兒子的大玩偶》，男主角坤樹最後在工作與兒子阿龍之間，為了兒子的歡喜，只好打消辭掉自己痛恨的小丑工作。

美國幽默小說家史塔頓正是運用了這一兩難的情節，寫下了一個沒有結局的故事：英俊的青年愛上了公主，卻得面對大審判，在他的面前有兩道門，一道門後面是美女的報酬；另一道門後面是作老虎的大餐，他會選擇哪一道？青年望向公主，因為她知道那兩扇門的祕密，他渴望公主給他暗示；公主心裡卻是掙扎萬分，她無法接受愛人與美女遠走高飛，重新生活，卻也不願看到愛人落入虎口，屍骨不存，所以她想了很久，終於微指右邊的門，青年於是走向右邊那扇門，也正當讀者屏息以待門打開的結果時候，故事竟結束了！是美女還是老虎？比歐亨利式更意外是，作者把答案的兩難留給了讀者去決定。

以筆者看法，公主介乎的兩難只是不甘的妒嫉與不捨愛人生命之間，兩難之間，道德、是非的差距太大，是個人小愛與大愛的距離，其實不難選擇，就兩難的張力言，較黃春明的《兒子的大玩偶》之感傷與無奈遠矣！

三、閱讀文選

The Lady Or The Tiger?

Frank Stockton

In the very olden time there lived a *semi—barbaric*（半野蠻的）king. He was a man of *exuberant fancy*（充滿活力的幻想），and, of *an authority so irresistible*（不可抗拒的權威）that, at his will, he turned his fancies into facts.

Among the exuberant and barbaric fancy, the *arena*（競技場）of the king was built as *an agent of justice*（司法的代表場所），in which crime was punished, or *rewarded*（報酬），by the *decrees*

（決定）of an *impartial and incorruptible*（公平、清廉）chance.

When a *subject*（人民）*was accused of*（被告）a crime of *sufficient*（足夠到）importance to interest the king that, the *fate*（命運）of the accused person would be decided in the king's arena on an appointed day. When all the people had *assembled in the galleries*（集合就座位）, and the king, on his *throne*（王位）, gave a signal, a door beneath him opened, and the accused subject stepped out into the *amphitheater*（古羅馬式的圓形競技場）. *Directly opposite*（直對面）him, there were two doors, exactly alike and side by side. It was the *privilege*（特有的權利）of the person on *trial*（審判）to walk directly to these doors and open one of them. He could open either door he pleased. If he opened the one, there came out of it a hungry tiger , would immediately *sprang upon*（撲上）him and *tore him to pieces*（撕成碎片）as a *punishment for his guilt*（罪懲）. But, if the accused person opened the other door, there came forth from it a lady, and to this lady he was immediately married, as a *reward of his innocence*（無罪的酬謝）.

This was the king's semi—barbaric method of *administering justice*（司法審理）. The *criminal*（罪犯）could not know out of which door would come the lady or tiger. The *institution*（制度）was a very popular one.

This semi—barbaric king had a daughter. As is usual in such cases, she was the apple of his eye, and was loved by him above all humanity. Among his *courtiers*（朝臣）was a young man who fell in love with the *princess*（公主）. The princess was *well satisfied with*（滿意）her lover, for he was handsome and brave to a degree *unsurpassed*（無人能及）in all this kingdom. This love affair moved on happily for many months, until one day the king happened to discover its existence. But the king would not think of allowing any fact of this kind to *interfere with*（干擾）the workings of the *tribunal*（裁判）. The youth was immediately *cast into*（丟進）prison, and a day was appointed for his trial in the king's arena.

The appointed day arrived. The king and his *court*（宮廷）were in their places. All was ready. The signal was given. A door beneath the royal party opened, and the lover of the princess walked into the arena. He turned, as the custom was, to *bow to*（鞠躬）the king, but his eyes were *fixed upon*（固定在）the princess, who sat to the right of her father. She knew in which of the two rooms, that stood the tiger, and in which waited the lady.

And not only did she know in which room stood the lady ready to *emerge*（出現）, but she knew who the lady was. It was one of the *fairest and loveliest*（最美麗與可愛的）of the court and the princess hated her.

When her lover turned and looked at her, and his eye met hers as she sat there. The only hope for the youth was based upon the success of the princess in discovering this mystery; and the moment he looked upon her, he saw she would succeed.

Then it was that his *quick and anxious glance*（焦慮渴望的一瞥）asked the question: "Which?" It was as *plain*（明白）to her *as if he shouted*（雖是眼光詢問卻有如大叫）it from where he stood. The question was asked in a *flash*（如電光石火間）; it must be answered in another. She raised her hand, and made a slight, quick movement toward the right. No one but her lover saw her. Every eye but his was fixed on the man in the arena.

He turned, and with a *firm and rapid step*（堅定與快速步伐）he walked across the empty space. Every heart stopped beating, every breath was held, every eye was fixed immovably upon that man. *Without the slightest hesitation*（毫不猶豫）, he went to the door on the right, and opened it.

Now, the point of the story is this: Did the tiger come out of that door, or did the lady ?

Would it not be better for him to die at once?

The question of her decision is not for me as the one person able to answer it. And so I leave it with all of you: Which came out of the opened door — the lady, or the tiger?

四、作品延伸作業

看來這故事還沒有完結，需要妳的想像力畫下句點，你可以有很多的角度去判斷：

一、右門後是美女，兩人從此幸福美滿的婚姻，就是結
　　局嗎？公主的反應呢？可就人性的陰暗或道德面去
　　想像。

二、就男子的心理去猜測？雖猜中公主心意，他會以死成
　　全？或……．

三、想像右門後的老虎反應？

四、想像國王的安排？

喬伊斯《伊芙琳》
——小說之蒙太奇大師

小說特徵
愛爾蘭鄉土情懷‧意識流
（Stream of Consciousness）

詹姆斯‧喬伊斯
(James Joyce, 1882–1941)

All the seas of the world tumbled about her heart. He was drawing her into them: he would drown her. She gripped with both hands at the iron railing.

-James Joyce, "Eveline"

世界所有的海水湧入她的內心。他正拉她入海，使她淹沒。她雙手緊抓鐵欄杆不放。

——喬伊斯〈伊芙琳〉

一、作者短評

　　詹姆斯‧喬伊斯（James Joyce），1882年，出生於愛爾蘭都柏林的富裕天主教家庭，但喬伊斯父親的酗酒以及理財的不善，家境旋由富裕變貧窮，在喬伊斯的小說中，常現的父親角色，正是他以自己父親形象之塑造。

　　喬伊斯大學畢業後到巴黎、蘇黎世等地過著流浪生活，1920年至1939年期間定居法國。儘管喬伊斯一生大部分時光都遠離故土愛爾蘭，但極重鄉土意識的他，他小說中故事的發生大多根植於他早年在都柏林的生活，包括他的家庭、朋友、敵人、中學和大學的歲月。喬伊斯早期出版的短篇小說集《都柏林人》（1914）就是深入剖析都柏林社會發展的遲緩和麻木，也從這部小說中，喬伊斯 意識流技巧，初露端倪，他運用大量心理獨白，而且更多的關注於人的內心世界而非客觀現實，深刻表達他的故土懷情。

　　喬伊斯最大文學成就是全面推進和發展意識流小說，帶領此一文學流派邁上顛峰。意識流小說是對尋常人物內心世界的複雜活動，提供更真實的描述，包括清醒的意識、無意識、夢幻意識和語言前意識，天馬行空，全然不受時空拘束的文學技巧。喬伊斯於1906年完成《都柏林人》之後的小說《尤利西斯》，意識流技巧最淋漓盡致，將古希臘神話融入現代文學的敘事結構，這部小說的全部故事情節都在都柏林的一天之內發生：1904年6月16日。《尤利西斯》全書分為18個章節，每個章節講述一天中一個小時之內發生的事，是意識流文學的極緻之作，樹立喬依思小說大師地位。

二、作品分析

　　現代主義小說中，意識流是一個特殊的學派，可說是小說寫創上極大之革新。意識流小說家對傳統小說中，作者當然主導角色的身世、內心與外界環境，有時還要挺身而出，對角色評頭論足，認為毫無必要；時空排列上，意識流也不循傳統小說時間與空間的直線編年。喬伊斯主張消滅作者人格的干預，認為沒有作者意識的作品是最高的美學形式，並力圖在小說中達到這一目標。

　　「意識流」最初見於美國心理學家威廉・詹姆斯，他認為人類的意識活動是一種連續不斷的流動狀態。20世紀初，弗洛伊德的下意識和夢與藝術關係的理論，都對意識流文學的發展有重大影響。由於其技巧獨特，意識流文學在概念與技巧上的特徵有（一）內心獨白：純粹是小說中人物自己把所感所思的內心意識，毫無顧忌的直接表露出來。（二）內心分析：對自己自然流動思想和感受，進行分析、探索。（三）自由聯想：任何能激發新的思緒與浮想，可不受任何規律和次序限制，都能打斷人物的思路，釋放一連串的印象和感觸。（四）時間和空間蒙太奇：意識流小說家，情節也不受時空的限制，表現意識流動的多變性、複雜性。

本文所挑選之《伊芙琳》（Eveline），是喬伊斯的短篇小說集《都柏林人》中的一篇，描繪都柏林人們的生活狀態，與這座城市的貧窮和枯燥，可謂細緻入微。內容敘述一位19歲少女伊芙琳不甘浪費生命，繼續蟄伏在沒落故鄉，就在決心與愛人法蘭克私奔前，卻又不捨故人鄉土，最後對故鄉愛爾蘭與家之眷念，初從家中窗簾布，想著為何有這麼多打掃不完的灰塵、幼時遊玩的大庭院、父親的兇悍、家務的操勞、商店同事的尖酸刻薄與母親一生的作牛作馬抱怨；但心情一轉，又對窗簾布氣味的眷戀，想到她在母親死前，答應照顧家庭的承諾，父親也有溫暖溫馨的時刻，內心起了猶豫不捨的心情，最後，在上船前的一刻，愛情與家人的拉扯心情像是驚濤駭浪，當下，她決定放棄離開這個家，對法蘭克有如大海襲來般的催促，伊芙琳只有回望法蘭克，「她的眼神沒有一絲愛戀或即將離別的跡象，也沒有曾經熟稔的表情。」，相較下，意識流的小說技巧大大勝出傳統寫法，更能探微人心細膩之活動，不談什麼大道理，就只有伊芙琳的內心的小世界流動，讓抽象的意識有了體溫、氣味與視覺，足夠會心一悟。

三、閱讀文選

Eveline

James Joyce

She sat at the window watching the evening *invade*（侵入）the *avenue*（街道）. Her head was *leaned against*（靠著）the *window curtains*（窗簾）and in her *nostrils*（鼻孔）was the *odor*（氣味）of *dusty cretonne*（滿佈灰塵窗簾布）. She was tired.

Few people passed. The man out of the last house passed on his way home; she heard his footsteps *crunching*（走路發出的嘎嘎聲）on the *cinder path*（煤渣路）before the new red houses. One time there *used to*（曾經）be a *field*（廣場）where they used to play every evening with other children—the Devines, the Waters, the Dunns, little Keogh the *cripple*（跛腳）, she and her brothers and sisters. Ernest, however, never played: he was too grown up. Her father often used to hunt them in out of the field with his *blackthorn stick*（藤條棍子）; but usually little Keogh *kept nix*（把風；警戒）and called out when he saw her father coming. Her father was not so bad then; and besides, her mother was alive. That was a long time ago. Tizzie Dunn was dead, too, and the Waters had gone back to England. Everything changes. Now she was going to go away like the others, to leave her home.

Home! She looked round the room, which she *had dusted*（打掃）once a week for so many years, *wondering*（驚訝；不解）

14 喬伊斯《伊芙琳》　　133

where on earth all the dust came from.

She had *consented to*（答應）go away, to leave her home. Was that *wise*（明智）? She tried to *weigh*（衡量）each side of the question. In her home anyway she had *shelter*（遮風躲雨處）and food. Of course she had to work hard, both in the house and at the Store. What would they say of her in the Stores when they found out that she had *run away with*（私奔）a fellow? Say she was a fool. Miss Gavan would be glad. She had always had an *edge*（尖酸刻薄）on her. She would not cry many tears at leaving the Stores.

But in her new home, in a *distant unknown*（遙遠不明的）country, it would not be like that. Then she would be married—she, Eveline. People would treat her with respect then. She would not be treated as her mother had been. Even now, though she was over nineteen, she sometimes felt herself in danger of her father's violence. And she had nobody to protect her. Her brothers—Ernest was dead and Harry, who was in the church *decorating*（裝潢）business, was nearly always down somewhere in the country. Besides, the *squabble*（爭吵）for money on Saturday nights had begun to *weary her unspeakably*（讓她無法言表的厭倦）. She always gave her *entire*（全部的）wages—seven *shillings*（先令；英國幣制）. But her father said she used to *squander*（糟蹋；浪費）the money that he was not going to give her his hard—earned money. In the end he would ask her buying Sunday's dinner. Then she had to *rush out as quickly as she could*（拼命急忙跑出去）and returned home late *under her load of provisions*（大包小包食物地回家）. It was hard work—a hard life—but now that she was about to leave it.

She was about to *explore*（探索）another life with Frank. Frank was very kind, manly, open—hearted. She was to go away with him to be his wife and to live with him in Buenos Ayres where he had a home waiting for her. How well she remembered the first time she had seen him; It seemed a few weeks ago. Then they had come to know each other. He used to meet her outside the Stores every evening and see her home.

He had started as a *deck boy*（船上甲板雜役）on a ship of the Allan Line going out to Canada. He told her the names of the ships he had been on. He had fallen on his feet in Buenos Ayres（布宜諾斯艾利斯，阿根廷首都）, he said, and had come over to the old country just for a holiday. Of course, her father had found out the *affair*（愛情）and had *forbidden*（禁止）her to have anything to say to him.

"I know these *sailor chaps*（水手傢伙）," he said.

One day he had *quarreled with*（爭吵）Frank and after that she had to meet her lover secretly.

The evening deepened in the avenue. In her *lap*（大腿）laid the white of two letters—one was to Harry; the other was to her father. Her father was becoming old lately, she noticed; he would miss her. Sometimes he could be very nice. Not long before, he had read her out a ghost story and made toast for her at the fire. Another day, when their mother was alive, they had all gone for a picnic to the Hill of Howth. She remembered her father putting on her mothers *bonnet*（無帶的女帽）to make the children laugh.

Her time was running out（時間將盡）but she continued to sit by the window, leaning her head against the window curtain, *inhaling*（吸著）the odor of dusty cretonne. Down far in the avenue she could hear a *street organ playing*（街頭的琴音）. She remembered the last night of her mother's illness; she heard the *melancholy*（憂鬱的）play. It *remind*（提醒) her *of* the promise to keep the home together as long as she could that very night .

As she *mused*（沉思）the pitiful *vision*（可憐的影像）of her mother's life, she stood up *in a sudden impulse of terror*（恐懼的衝動）. Escape! She must escape! Frank would save her. He would give her life, perhaps love, too. She had a right to happiness. Frank would take her in his arms, fold her in his arms. He would save her.

She stood among the *swaying*（晃動）crowd in the station at the North Wall. He held her hand and she knew that he was speaking to her over and over again. She *caught a glimpse of*（瞟了一眼）the boat. She answered nothing. She felt her cheek pale and cold and she prayed to God to direct her, to show her what was her duty. If she went, tomorrow she would be on the sea with Frank, steaming towards Buenos Ayres. Their *passage*（航程）had been *booked*（已預訂）. Could she still draw back after all he had done for her?

A bell *clanged upon*（敲擊聲）her heart. She felt him *seize*（抓住）her hand:

"Come!"

All the seas of the world *tumbled about*（翻騰）her heart. He was drawing her into them: he would *drown*（淹死）her. She *gripped with both hands at*（雙手緊抓）the iron railing.

"Come!"

"Eveline! Evvy!"

He rushed beyond *the barrier*（攔障）and called to her to follow. She set her white face to him, *passive*（冷淡）, like a helpless animal. Her eyes gave him no sign of love or farewell or *recognition*（認出，喻不曾相識）.

四、作品延伸作業

　　喬伊斯的《伊芙琳》離家的內心掙扎，或伍爾芙《一間鬼屋》一個人「寶藏」的追求，意識流小說家靠意識流動的多變性、複雜性，突破時空的限制，來暗示人物在某一「瞬間」的感受、印象、精神狀態或作品寓意。

　　利用事實、回憶和幻想、個人潛意識的的穿插，妳可以如夢似幻、天馬行空、不受傳統文法拘束的寫出妳自己最有感，個人獨特的私密性創作。

伍爾芙《一間鬼屋》
——內心更潛深處之探索

小說特徵

性別、女權與意識流

弗吉尼亞‧伍爾芙
（Virginia Woolf 1882 –1941）

A woman must have money and a room of her own if she is to write fiction.

-Virginia Woolf

女性若是想要寫作，一定要有錢和自己的房間（空間）。

——弗吉尼亞‧伍爾芙

一、作者短評

　　小說家之異於常人者，不外敏銳過人，多愁善感，「衣帶漸寬終不悔，為伊銷得人憔悴」，伍爾芙即此極端之例。在失去正常女人親情、愛情以至婚姻、家庭的代價下，伍爾芙一生受憂鬱症折磨，生活如在火山熔岩翻騰的精神煉獄中，卻煅煉出如晶如鑽之作品，大放人世光芒。

　　弗吉尼亞·伍爾芙（Virginia Woolf），英國女作家，也是現代主義與女性主義的先鋒之一。她和詹姆斯·喬伊斯，公認是二十世紀意識流成就最高的作家，巧合是兩人也是生死同年，運用意識流的寫作方法，去描繪沉底人心的潛意識，極大地影響了傳統的小說寫作手法，為傳統文學和現代文學劃下分水嶺。

　　伍爾芙出身書香門第，家世顯赫，自幼精神脆弱，卻天性敏感，具有不可思議的理解力和敏銳觀察的邏輯，她幾乎可以看到別人的內心深處，寫出那些別人無法表達出來的奧秘想法，這也許是她會成為意識流小說大家的原因，但也不知當感謝還是該憐惜，伍爾芙一生就在精神崩潰，憂鬱症折磨的狀態下，寫出不朽作品。

　　伍爾芙對於別人有關她作品的評價極為敏感，甚至到了神經質的狀態，由於她的精神分裂症狀越來越嚴重，她在自傳《存在的瞬間》（Moments of Being）中透露了小時候受到家庭性侵，讓她的身心受到極大摧殘，心中留下陰影，以致她一生厭惡性行為，不願生育，不和丈夫同房。1941年3月28日，伍爾芙毫無留戀，一步一步向河中心走去，慢慢地沉入了河水深處，結束了自己煎熬的一生。艾略特（T.S. Eliot）認為伍爾芙是當時英國文學的中心，是一種文明模式的代表。她的逝世意味着一個時代的結束。

二、作品分析

　　伍爾芙與其他男性意識流作家不同之處在於，她的小說往往富有詩意，在語言上更像詩體散文，富有唯美主義的情調，描寫單位由社群轉至個人，由外部感官導入內部知覺，由生理移向心理，其敘事觀點也由第三人稱的全知轉成全面的心理獨白，時空自由穿梭，發展出一個獨立的虛構世界；其內在獨白之深邃，所傳達出個人內心複雜的感受，是意識流的高峰之作，但其小說內容的晦澀難懂卻和其他意識流作家的作品別無二致。在其代表作《一間鬼鳥》中，雖原文是僅六、七百字的短篇小說，但乍讀十分晦澀省略，情節極少，主詞或省略受詞的敘述，所以大量使用「分詞構句」，她的代名詞也是模糊困惑不知指誰。

　　《一間鬼鳥》中，伍爾芙高明的安排在一間屋內，卻是陰、陽兩界，一生一死的兩對夫婦男女，彼此的相互觀察與互動，主題則是一對百年前死亡，重回舊巢的男女鬼魂，尋找屋中的寶藏。從故事一開始，只見男女鬼魂到處遊蕩，到故事中間，我們知道了他們在尋找埋藏許久的「寶物」，最後一句話，終於告訴我們寶物是甚麼。

伍爾芙為意識流更創新境，以屋中的一面的玻璃窗戶，隔開了陰、陽兩界的動線，像不像印象畫派光影視覺的文字享受，讓這間房子有了栩栩如生的心跳，直到這對鬼魂夫婦凝視屋中夫婦安祥的沉睡狀態，才找到了屋中的寶藏，就是昔日兩人共處歡樂無憂的美好時光！

三、閱讀文選

A Haunted House

Virginia Woolf

Whatever hour you woke there was a *door shutting*（門正在關上）. From room to room they went, hand in hand, *lifting here, opening there,*（比喻東碰碰，西摸摸，在尋找某物）making sure—*a ghostly couple*（一對鬼夫妻）. "*Here we left it,*（我們（把東西）留在這裡）" she said. And he added, "Oh, but here too!" "It's upstairs," she *murmured*（喃喃自語）. "And in the garden," he *whispered*（小聲）"Quietly," they said, "*or we shall wake them.*"（不要吵醒他們——這是一對活夫妻）

But it was not that you woke us. ….. the house all empty, the doors standing open, only the wood pigeons *bubbling with content*（愉快的咕嚕聲）and *the hum of the threshing machine*（打穀機的嗡嗡聲）sounding from the farm. "What did I come in here for? What did I want to find?" My hands were empty. "Perhaps it's upstairs then?" The apples were in the *loft*（閣樓）. And so down again, the garden still as ever, only the book had *slipped into*（滑落到）the grass.

Not that one could ever see them. The *window panes*（窗戶的玻璃）*reflected*（映射出）apples, reflected roses; all the leaves were green in the glass. If they moved in the *drawing room*（客廳）, the apple only turned its yellow side. The shadow of a *thrush*（畫眉鳥）crossed the *carpet*（地毯）; from the *deepest wells of silence*（寂靜的深井中）the wood pigeon drew its bubble of sound. "Safe, safe, safe," the *pulse*（脈搏；心跳聲）of the house beat softly. "The treasure *buried*（埋藏）; the room..." Oh, was that the buried treasure?

A moment later the light had *faded*（衰退）. Death was the glass; death was between us; coming to the woman first, hundreds of years ago, leaving the house, sealing all the windows; the rooms were darkened. He left it, left her, went North, went East, saw the stars turned in the Southern sky; sought the house, found it dropped beneath *the Downs*（英國東南部牧羊丘陵草原地）. "Safe, safe, safe," the pulse of the house beat gladly. "The Treasure yours."

The wind *roars*（呼嘯過）up the avenue. Trees *stoop and bend*（俯身彎屈）this way and that. *Moonbeams*（月光）*splash and spill*（四散飛濺）wildly in the rain. But the *beam of the lamp*（路燈的光線）falls straight from the window. The candle burns *stiff and still*（靜止不動）. *Wandering*（徘徊）through the house, opening the windows, whispering not to wake us, the ghostly couple seek their joy.

"Here we slept," she says. And he adds, "Kisses without number." "Waking in the morning—" "*Silver between the trees*（樹木間的銀光閃爍）—" "Upstairs—" "In the garden—" "When summer came—" "In winter snowtime—" The doors go shutting far in the distance, gently knocking like the pulse of a heart.

Nearer they come; cease at the doorway. Our eyes darken; we hear no steps beside us; we see no lady *spread her ghostly cloak*（掀動女鬼的斗篷）. His hands *shield*（遮住）the lantern. "Look," he breathes. "Sound asleep. Love upon their lips."

Stooping（彎著腰）, holding their silver lamp above us, long they look and deeply. Long they pause. The wind drives straightly; the flame stoops slightly. Wild beams of moonlight cross both floor and wall; the faces *pondering*（思考）; the faces that *search*（察覺）the sleepers and seek their hidden joy.

"Safe, safe, safe," the heart of the house beats proudly. "Long years—" he *sighs*（歎息）. "Again you found me." "Here," she murmurs, "sleeping; in the garden reading; laughing, rolling apples in the loft. Here we left our treasure—" "Safe! safe! safe!" the pulse of the house beats wildly. "Oh, is this buried treasure? The light in the heart."

16 馬克・吐溫《好小孩的故事》
——美國西部文學之幽默大師

小說特徵

美國西部風土、人情的口語
化幽默

馬克・吐溫
（Mark Twain, 1835 –1910）

Humor is the great thing, the saving thing. The minute it crops up, all our irritations and resentments slip away and a sunny spirit takes their place.

-Mark Twain

幽默是最棒的事，是救人的東西。當幽默一來，我們所有的憤怒
與不滿都會走開，一個充滿陽光的精神會取而代之。

——馬克・吐溫

一、作者短評

　　馬克‧吐溫，原名山姆．克萊門斯（Samuel Langhorne Clemens），1835年，出生於美國密蘇里州的小城佛羅里達（Florida），在他4歲的時候，全家遷往緊鄰密西西比河畔的小鎮漢尼拔（Hannibal），他日後小說《湯姆歷險記》（The Adventures of Tom Sawyer）和《哈克芬恩歷險記》（Adventures of Huckleberry Finn）的靈感素材，即來自這個密西西比河港小鎮的風土人情。

　　所謂「靠山吃山，靠水吃水」，馬克吐溫生來與密西西比河為伍，對這條隔開東岸，象徵大西部的大河，情感濃厚。馬克吐溫自小立志當個汽船領航員，「馬克吐溫」靈感即來自密西西比河上測水人的術語，意指「水深兩潯」（two fathoms：約3.7米）。二十三歲時，他終於取得了正式領航員的資格，但沒多久，南北戰爭開始，密西西比河的航行中斷，馬克‧吐溫失去了領航員的職務。由於密蘇里州恰處美國南北界標的模糊地帶，居民應屬南軍或北軍，莫衷一是，馬克‧吐溫後來雖被劃歸南軍，但只當了兩星期的南軍便「落跑」，旋即到西部淘金，歷盡大平原、洛磯山脈、甚至猶他州之鹽湖城，一年後，無功而返，轉行進入新聞報業，而這些美國大西部之所見所聞，正好提供了他日後踏入文壇的寫作能量。馬克吐溫直率、口語化幽默的文筆，大受人民歡迎，瞬間，取得全國性的名氣，樹立馬克吐溫的文豪地位。馬克吐溫於一八六五年十月，寫信給他弟弟信中談到了他決心接受「上帝的召喚」，去從事

「上帝要他作的事」，換言之，即是寫幽默文學，透過笑聲來鼓舞人類精神，帶動人正面的生活能量。

這位代表美國文學象徵的馬克吐溫出生時，恰逢哈雷彗星劃越地球，彷彿他是來自天上的賀禮，馬克吐溫因此一直以為他也會乘哈雷彗星而去，1910年4月21日，馬克吐溫在美國康乃狄格州因心臟病去世，一天後，哈雷彗星果然再度光臨地球，劃空而去，彷彿接走在人間75年的馬克吐溫，重歸天際。

二、作品分析

國與國，因地理之不同，自生文化之差異。其實，一國之內因地域之有別，亦有風土人情之不同。美國地域的爭議，我們一般將注意力放在南北方向，但在南北差異之餘，美國也有東西的文化差別，只是他們不同南北問題那樣的火爆與激烈，相較極端，自易引人矚目——像是對黑白種族、經濟宗教或自由保守的見解。馬克吐溫正是深刻注意到東、西部文化不同的作家，他對美國大西部純樸、直接的泥土味，一直認為是保有美國獨立精神的理想夢奇地，而西部的美國人——豪邁、粗獷、不拘禮節的個性，更被馬克吐溫認定是忠於原味的美國人，深深有別於在文明禮俗調教（tamed）後的東部美國人。

馬克吐溫1865年的成名之作《坎拉貝斯城有名的跳蛙》，即著筆東部文明與西部拓荒地兩者之間的價值衝突，故事主體暗喻對東部的道德諷刺，敘述一位樂觀、心地單純的西部賭徒史邁利，在一場「跳蛙」比賽中，敗給了使詐來自東部人，不論是形容賽馬、鬥狗與跳蛙的動作，如「青蛙在空中躍騰如同旋轉的甜圈圈、落地如貓」，以及東部人使詐將鉛彈灌進跳蛙嘴巴的技倆，比賽時，跳蛙挺了一下「聳起肩膀—活像個法國人，毫無用處—像教堂一樣穩固，膠著在那裏」，這種對獨特細節具體用心化諸口語式幽默文學，讓故事的喜感效果，引人捧腹。馬克吐溫就是以幽默的態度敘事，而不是嚴厲地去描繪文化上的對立，讓他小說更加引人入勝。

本書所選同時寫於1865年的《好小孩的故事》，馬克吐溫以坦白、嘲諷、誇張幽默的筆調，敘述一位孩童Jacob Blivens，他循規蹈矩，行為品性好到離譜，卻顯得食古不化，所有同齡小孩平常打彈子、抓鳥到調皮、惡作劇的事一概不作，Jacob堅守主日學的教條，不但要作最乖的小孩，還要教導壞小孩（bad boys）改邪歸正，結果 Jacob Blivens下場的根本不是書本教的那回事，他要壞小孩不要偷摘蘋果，壞小孩跌下來卻是壓傷他；他制止壞小孩偷玩帆船，結果自己跌下水，他用所有老師稱讚的介紹信應徵船員，被船長奚落不切實際，最後好小孩在制止壞小孩逗弄狗時被炸得粉身碎骨，「Jacob穿過屋頂，飛向太揚，後連著十五條狗的身體殘餘，就像風箏後面的尾穗一般」，全文充滿美國西部人豪放、不在乎的語調，暗諷現代文明與宗教的教條，讓小孩失去了最可愛的童稚與赤子之心，不斷讓讀者腦海浮現出《湯姆歷險記》中，那位靈活、頑皮，一身是膽的西部小孩，才是馬克吐溫渴望的美國少年典型。

三、閱讀文選

The Story of the Good Little Boy

Mark Twain

Once there was a good little boy by the name of Jacob Blivens. He always *obeyed*（服從；孝順）his parents, no matter how *absurd and unreasonable*（荒唐與不合理的）their demands were; and he always learned his book, and never was late at Sabbath—school. None of the other boys could ever make that boy out. He couldn't lie, no matter how convenient it was. And he was so honest that he was simply ridiculous. He wouldn't play *marbles*（彈珠）on Sunday, he wouldn't rob birds' nests, he wouldn't give *hot pennies*（燒燙的銅板）to *organ—grinders'*（街頭手風琴手；暗喻乞丐）monkeys; he didn't seem to take any interest in any kind of *amusement*（娛樂；好玩的事）. So the other boys used to try to reason it out, but they couldn't arrive at any satisfactory conclusion.

This good little boy read all the *Sunday—school books*（主日學課本；專為小朋友星期日上教堂查經的書）; they were his greatest *delight*（快樂）. Jacob had a *noble ambition*（高尚的企圖）to be like those good little boys with pictures put in the Sunday—school books. He *longed to come across*（期望遇到）one of them alive once; but he never did. They all died before his time, maybe. It made him *feel a little uncomfortable*（感到不太舒

服）sometimes when he *reflected*（思索）that the good little boys always died. He loved to live. So at last, he made up his mind to *do the best*（盡力）to live right, and *have his dying speech all ready when his time came*（準備好他的臨死前的感言）.

But somehow nothing ever went right with this good little boy, and it all happened just the other way. When he found Jim Blake stealing apples, and went under the tree to warn him about a bad little boy who fell out of a neighbor's apple tree and broke his arm, Jim fell out of the tree, too, but he fell on him and broke his arm, and Jim wasn't hurt at all. Jacob couldn't understand that. There wasn't anything in the books like it.

And once, when Jacob found a *lame dog*（瘸腿狗）that hadn't any place to stay, and was hungry and *persecuted*（被虐待）, he brought him home and fed him, but when he was going to *pet*（寵物）him the dog *flew at* him and tore all the clothes off him. It was of the *same breed of dogs*（同類種的狗）that was in the books, but it acted very differently. The very things *the boys got in the books* （由書本中所學的東西）*rewarded to be the most unprofitable things*（回報是毫無助益）.

Once, when he was on his way to Sunday—school, he saw some bad boys pleasuring in a sailboat（帆船）. He was filled with *consternation*（驚慌）, because he knew from his reading that boys who went sailing on Sunday *got drowned*（淹死）. So he ran out on a *raft*（木筏）to warn them, but *a log*（圓木）*slid him into the river*（滑過來衝撞入河）. A man got him out pretty soon, and the doctor *pumped*（擠壓出）the water out of him, but he caught cold and lay sick abed nine weeks. But *the most unaccountable thing*（最不解的事）about it was that the bad boys in the boat had a good time all day, and then reached home alive and well.

When he got well he was a little *discouraged*（氣餒）, but he *resolved to*（決心）keep on trying anyhow. He found that it was now time for him to go to sea as a cabin—boy. He called on a ship—captain and *made his application*（提出申請）, and when the captain asked for his *recommendations*（推薦）he proudly *drew out compliment*（長篇大論讚美）from a teacher, on a *tract*（小冊子）, had *never failed to move*（從沒不感動）ship—captains, and open the way to all offices of honor in any book that ever he had read. But the captain was a *vulgar*（粗魯）man, and he said, "Oh, that be *blowed*（Damn的婉轉字）! That wasn't any proof that he knew how to wash dishes." This was altogether the most *extraordinary*（不尋常的）thing that ever happened to Jacob in all his life. He could hardly believe his senses.

This boy always had a hard time of it. At last, one day, when he was around *hunting up*（尋獵）bad little boys to *admonish*（訓話）, he found a lot of them in the old *iron—foundry*（鐵工廠）, which they had *tied*（綁住）fourteen or fifteen dogs together *in long procession*（一長列）, and were going to *fix with nitroglycerin cans to their tails*（固定炸藥罐在尾巴上）. Jacob sat down on one of those cans, and he took hold of（抓住）the foremost dog by the collar. But just at that moment Alderman（市議員）McWelter, full of *wrath*（憤怒）, stepped in. All the bad boys ran away, but Jacob Blivens rose in *conscious innocence*（問心無愧）. But the man took Jacob Blivens by the ear and turned him around, and hit him with *the flat of his hand*（手掌）; and *in an instant*（瞬間）that good little boy *shot out through the roof*（炸穿屋頂）and *soared away toward*（飄向）the sun, with the *fragments*（碎屍）of those fifteen dogs stringing after him like *the tail of a kite*（風箏尾穗）. And there wasn't a sign of that alderman or that old iron—foundry left on the face of the earth; and, as for young Jacob Blivens, he never got a chance to make his last dying speech, *unless*（除非）he made it to the birds; because, although the *bulk*（屍骨）of him came down all right in a tree—top in an *adjoining*（鄰近）county, *the rest of him was apportioned around*（其餘分佈）among four townships. You never saw a boy *scattered so*（這樣四分五裂的飛散）.

Thus *perished*（死去）the good little boy who did the best he could, but didn't come out according to the books. Every boy who ever did as he did *prospered*（功成名就）except him. His case is truly remarkable. It will probably never be *accounted for*（解釋）.

四、作品延伸作業

鄉土、直接的口語幽默，讓人讀得開心又會心，是馬克吐溫作品的風格迷人與受人歡迎的關鍵，台灣地方作家黃春明先生也堪稱代表：閱讀《兒子的大玩偶》與《蘋果的滋味》。

威廉·福克納《給愛蜜麗的玫瑰》
——美國南方社會文學小説家

小説特徵

美國南方風土、種族、人情的寫實

威廉·福克納
(William Faulkner, 1897－1962)

There is no mechanical way to get the writing done, no shortcut. The young writer would be a fool to follow a theory. Teach yourself by your own mistakes; people learn only by error.

-William C. Faulkner

一部作品的完成其實沒有固定方式或捷徑。愚昧的年輕作家只會服從理論，卻不知從錯誤中學習，自己的錯誤才是良師。

——威廉·福克納

一、作者短評

　　威廉·福克納（William Cuthbert Faulkner），1897年，生於密西西比州的新奧爾巴尼（New Albany），當他四歲的時候，全家搬到了牛津鎮（Oxford），福克納終生待在美國南方成長、寫作，深受南方傳統風土人情的影響，大多數作品皆以他的故鄉密西西比為背景，像牛津鎮就是他的小說《獻給愛蜜麗的玫瑰》中傑佛遜鎮的構想原型。福克納被認為是美國最重要的南方作家之一，他的作品中有南方人特有性情，深入刻畫南方地位、矛盾等敏感問題，生動描繪出惟妙惟肖的南方人形象。

　　福克納筆下的劇情浸染著人物的複雜心理變化，綿延婉轉的感情描寫和反覆推敲的精巧措詞與海明威簡潔明瞭、乾脆利落的作品風格，是兩個極端。一般認為他是最出色美國現代主義作家，福克納多才多藝，作品範圍廣泛，像他《喧嘩與騷動》（The Sound and the Fury）是優秀的意識流作品，但福克納並不是純粹的意識流作家，他的大部分小說創作仍隸屬於寫實主義範疇，他也是多產的短篇小說家，有《給愛蜜麗的玫瑰》、《紅葉》（Red Leaves）、《夕陽》（That Evening Sun）。1940年，福克納一度前往好萊塢，專著於電影劇本寫作。

　　福克納一生浸泡在酒精之中，即便在1949年，諾貝爾文學獎典禮前，仍喝得酩酊大醉，說道：「我拒絕認為人類已經走到了盡頭……人類能夠忍受艱難困苦，也終將會獲勝。」卻是諾貝爾文學獎最精彩的感言之一。福克納從1957年起擔任維吉尼亞大學的駐校作家，1959年因騎馬摔下，重傷脊髓，從此苦於傷痛，直到1962年去世，年65。

二、作品分析

　　威廉福克納《給愛蜜麗的玫瑰》，讀者直接最大疑問就是作者以玫瑰為題，為什麼文章中，卻沒有寫到太多與玫瑰有關連性的內容呢？以福克納對南方獨特的情感與玫瑰高尚不群的優雅特徵，如要將這篇小說的主題與玫瑰作情理聯想，此一玫瑰，當是福克納經由愛蜜麗的生命經歷，象徵性的影射出他所要表達美國南方的不變與不同。這種表達方式，由莎士比亞「羅密歐與茱麗葉」悲劇裡的一段話，可以得到最好的意會：當茱麗葉愛上自己家族世仇的羅密歐時，他懷疑羅密歐的姓名有何意義。她說：「那朵我們稱為玫瑰的花，若換成別的名字，也是一樣芬芳。」

　　福克納標題用了玫瑰的意象來描述愛蜜麗的故事，間接表達南方文化的處境待遇。愛蜜麗的不幸乃是她對時代的變化，無動於衷，因此，她拒絕納稅，家中積滿塵埃，愛蜜麗在父親還沒有死之前，被教育的不得拋頭露面，沒有正常的社交，愛蜜麗的父親不只不和鎮上的人連絡，甚至還和親戚朋友斷絕了關係。這使生活有如在封閉鎖國的艾蜜莉，父親死後，曾經長達有三天，不相信父親的死去，甚至阻止鎮上的人幫忙。主題中蘊含了對六〇年代南方傳統、保守固執的遺憾，這一感慨，尤為強烈暗示在愛蜜麗愛上了來自北方到鎮上打工的現代年輕人荷馬，而當荷馬欲棄她而去，愛蜜麗為了保住尊嚴或是愛人，用砒霜將他毒死，保藏在房中，寧可與代表死亡的荷馬屍體，沉睡一生。

也許愛蜜莉所希冀的那朵玫瑰，正是她個人終於得有一個屬於自己甜蜜的新生花園，然而這場戀愛，終究在南方保守風氣，人言可畏下，謠傳荷馬是同性戀，加上愛蜜麗毫無處理愛情的智商下，而宣告破滅，而在那破滅之後，剩下則是佔有慾望的獨存，可憐愛蜜麗，這朵被種在溫室的玫瑰呀！

三、閱讀文選

A Rose for Emily

William Faulkner

When Miss Emily Grierson died, our whole town went to her funeral, mostly *out of curiosity*（出於好奇）to see the inside of her house, which no one *save*（除了）an old man—servant had seen in at least ten years.

Alive, Miss Emily had been a tradition, a duty, and a care; *a sort of hereditary obligation upon the town*（小鎮的一種世代義務）, *dating from*（日期溯自）that day in 1894 when Colonel Sartoris, the mayor *remitted her taxes*（免稅）. Colonel Sartoris *invented*（虛構）a tale *to the effect that*（按以下的意思）Miss Emily's father had *loaned*（借款）money to the town, which the town preferred this way of *repaying*（償還）.

When *the next generation*（下一代）, with its more modern ideas, became mayors and *aldermen*（市議員）, this arrangement created some little *dissatisfaction*（不滿）. On the first of the year they mailed her a tax notice. February came, and there was no reply. They called a special meeting of the Board of Aldermen（市鎮議會）. A *deputation*（代表團）knocked at the door through which no visitor had passed since she *ceased giving china painting lessons*（停止教授陶瓷繪畫課）eight or ten years earlier. They were *admitted*（引進）by the old Negro into a *dim hall*（昏暗矇矓的大廳）. The Negro led them into the *parlor*（會客室）.

They rose when she entered—a small, fat woman in black, with a thin gold chain. Her eyes looked like two small pieces of *coal*（煤炭）. She did not ask them to sit.

Her voice was dry and cold. "I have no taxes in Jefferson. Colonel Sartoris explained it to me. Perhaps one of you can *gain access to the city records*（去找市政紀錄查證）and satisfy yourselves."

So she *vanquished them*（說得他們落荒而逃）. That was two years after her father's death and a short time after her sweetheart—the one we believed would marry her —had *deserted*（拋棄）her. After her father's death she went out very little; after her sweetheart went away, people hardly saw her at all.

….., so they were not surprised when *the smell developed*（發出一股怪味）. A neighbor, a woman, complained to the mayor, Judge Stevens, eighty years old.

Judge Stevens said. "It's probably just a snake or a *rat*（老鼠）

that *nigger*（黑鬼）of hers killed in the yard. I'll speak to him about it."

The next day he received two more complaints. One said "I'd be the last one in the world to bother Miss Emily, but we've got to do something." So the next night, after midnight, four men crossed Miss Emily's lawn like *burglar*（闖空門的小偷）. They broke open the *cellar door*（地下室）and *sprinkled lime*（撒石灰）there, and in all the *outbuildings*（室外）. As they recrossed the lawn, a window that had been dark was lighted and Miss Emily sat in it, the light behind her, and her *upright torso motionless*（挺直不動的驅幹）as that of an idol.

That was when people had begun to feel really sorry for her. None of the young men were quite good enough for Miss Emily. We had long thought of them as a *tableau*（暗喻：活化石）.

When her father died, the house was all that was left to her; and in a way, people were glad. At last they could pity Miss Emily. Being left alone, she had become humanized.

The day after his death all the ladies prepared to call at the house, as is our *custom*（按照習俗）. Miss Emily met them at the door, dressed as usual and *with no trace of grief*（無絲毫的哀傷）on her face. She told them that her father was not dead. She did that for three days. Just as they were about to resort to law and force, she *broke down*（崩潰）, and they *buried*（埋葬）her father quickly.

She was sick for a long time. When we saw her again, her hair was cut short, making her look like a girl, with *a resemblance to those angels in colored church windows*（類似教堂窗戶的天使）—*sort of tragic and serene*（帶著悲劇與平靜的樣子）.

The town had just let the contracts for paving the sidewalks, and in the summer after her father's death they began the work. With the *construction company*（建設公司）came a *foreman*（工頭）

named Homer Barron, a Yankee—big, dark, with a big voice and eyes lighter than his face. Whenever you heard a lot of laughing anywhere about the square, Homer Barron would be in the center of the group. *Presently*（不久）we began to see him and Miss Emily on Sunday afternoons driving in the yellow—wheeled *buggy*（馬車）.

And as soon as the old people said, "Poor Emily," the whispering began. "Do you suppose it's really so?" they said to one another. "Of course, a Grierson would not think seriously of a *Northerner*（北方人）, a day laborer. Poor Emily."

She carried her head high enough—even when we believed that she was fallen. It was as if she demanded more than ever the recognition of her dignity as the last Grierson. Like when she bought the *rat poison*（毒鼠藥）, the *arsenic*（砒霜）. That was over a year after they had begun to say "Poor Emily ".

When she opened the package at home there was written on the box, under the *skull and bones*（骷髏；危險符號）: "For rats."

When she had first begun to be seen with Homer Barron, we had said, "She will marry him." We learned that Miss Emily had been to the jeweler's and ordered a man's *toilet set*（梳妝用具）in silver, with the letters H. B. on each piece. Two days later we learned that she had bought a complete outfit of men's clothing, including a nightshirt, and we said, "They are married."

And that was the last we saw of Homer Barron. And of Miss Emily for some time. Now and then we would see her at a window for a moment, but for almost six months she did not appear on the streets. From that time on her front door remained closed, save for a period of six or seven years, when she was about forty, during which she gave lessons in china—painting. The front door closed upon the last one and remained closed forever . When the town *got free postal* delivery（進行免費的郵遞）, Miss Emily alone refused to let them *fasten*（固定安裝）the *metal numbers*（門排號）above her door and a*ttach*（裝設）a mailbox to it.

Now and then（時常）we would see her in one of the downstairs windows—she had *evidently*（顯然）shut up the top floor of the house—*like the carved idol in a niche*（像是壁縫裏的雕像）, looking or not looking at us, we could never tell which.

And so she died. *Fell ill*（生病）in the house *filled with*（滿佈）dust and shadows, with only a Negro man to wait on her. She died in one of the downstairs rooms, in a heavy *walnut*（胡桃木）bed with a curtain, her gray head *propped on*（支撐在）a pillow yellow and with age and lack of sunlight.

They held the funeral on the second day. Already we knew that there was one room above stairs which no one had seen in forty years, and which would have to be forced. They waited until Miss Emily was in the ground before they opened it.

The violence of breaking down the door seemed to fill this room with *pervading*（漫佈）dust. ... everywhere upon this room *decked and furnished*（裝飾與家俱擺設）as for a *bride*（新娘）. Among them lay a collar and tie. Upon a chair hung the suit, *carefully folded*（細心地折疊）; beneath it the two mute shoes and the socks.

The man himself lay in the bed.

For a long while we just stood there, looking down at the body, had *apparently once laid in the attitude of an embrace*（顯然曾經有被擁抱過的姿勢躺臥）. Then we noticed that in the second *pillow*（枕頭）was *the indentation of a head*（有頭曾睡過的凹陷）. One of us *lifted*（拿起）something from it, and we saw a long strand of iron—gray hair.

四、作品延伸作業

威廉福克納《給愛蜜麗的玫瑰》是一部層次多面的小說：

一、對美國南方有什麼暗喻？

二、對美國南方女性的生活有什麼暗喻？

18 凱特・蕭邦《一小時的故事》 ——美國女性主義小說先驅

小說特徵
美國女性主義與女權

凱特・蕭邦
(Kate Chopin, 1851–1904)

When she abandoned herself a little whispered word escaped her slightly parted lips. She said it over and over under the breath: "free, free, free!"

"Free! Body and soul free!" she kept whispering.

-Kate Chopin, The Story of An Hour

當馬勒夫人放空自己，她微張的雙唇，重覆悄聲輕吐「自由、自由、自由！」

「自由！靈魂與肉體的自由！」，她持續低聲說著。

——凱特・蕭邦《一小時的故事》

一、作者短評

凱特・蕭邦（Kate Chopin），本名凱薩琳・歐福拉赫蒂（Katherine O'Flaherty），1851年，生於美國南方路易斯安那，是法國系克里歐人（Creole），蕭邦在作品中處處表達她對女性的關懷，公認為19世紀美國女性主義作家的先驅。

凱特蕭邦超越當時文學傳統和社會風氣紅線，專事女性主義題材寫作，顛覆了十九世紀美國社會對中產階級婦女「家庭小說」中「純真女性」的期待與規範，作品著重婦女在事業、婚姻、道德和心理方面的問題，尤其是女性追求自我渴望時所面臨的困境。1890年她發表第一部長篇小說《困惑》，是美國最早觸及離婚問題的小說。她筆下更試圖描繪出十九世紀女性內心的生理世界與矛盾不定的心情，作品《暴風雨》（The Tempest）赤裸寫出女性在情慾裡體驗到快樂的一面。

1899年長篇小說《覺醒》（Awakening）出版，此書是凱特最知名的作品，內容是關於一個不滿婚姻生活的妻子，她透過書中的女主角追求自我、愛情、獨立卻最後自殺的悲劇，大膽地描寫了婦女自我意識和性意識的覺醒，與美國當時保守氛圍大為衝突，這使蕭邦受到社會長期的冷落、責備，心情沮喪，抑鬱而逝。

凱特蕭邦短篇小說中以《一小時的故事》（The Story of An Hour）最為經典。隨著六〇年代女權運動興起，被冷落將近半世紀的凱特・蕭邦才又被重新發現，成為美國女性主義文學中的重要作家。

二、作品分析

　　筆者上課時，常愛問學生的一個問題就是——美國人和歐洲人，誰比較保守？誰較開放？也許好萊塢電影或美國媒體的強勢，往往大部學生選擇美國人較開放，但答案正好相反。因此，在分析凱特・蕭邦的《一個小時的故事》前，簡略談一下女性在美國社會地位的演進，順帶說明美國民族性的保守。

　　美國號稱以人權立國，1776年《獨立宣言》中，最響亮的一句話就是「人生而平等」（All men are created equal. 但這個 "men" 看來是不包括 "women"），美國人為此理想而發動獨立戰爭。1861年，美國人為此理想，再不惜內戰，犧牲六十萬生命，解放黑奴，也因此，當1863年，黑人都已取得公民地位時，美國女性仍不具有財產、教育及參政權，美國女性是直到1920年時，才得有最基本的投票權。

　　二十世紀前，美國女性在社會兩性地位上，可說是隱性到幾乎是隱形了。美國女性地位之卑微與美國清教（Puritans）的傳統大有關係，由霍桑的《紅字》，就可看出傳統上，女人就是男性的附屬品，女人一旦結婚，財產就歸丈夫所有，女性的一生職場就在家庭，最偉大的志業就是生兒育女，相夫教子，稍有見識女子，則視之女巫、異端，而有所謂「獵女巫」（Witch Hunting），殘酷者，以火燒死。美國民族性之保守，即便2004年民主黨的希拉蕊及歐巴馬爭逐總統候選大位時，美國人在面臨第一個女性總統或第一個黑人總統抉擇時，美國人還是寧可選取後者，由此可知，由保守向自由前進一步之維艱！

　　凱特・蕭邦在《一小時的故事》（The Story of An Hour），敘述馬勒夫人在一小時中，所歷經兩次心情震撼。丈夫火車意外的死訊，讓馬勒夫人帶來「當然」的悲痛，但在剎那間，馬勒夫人壓抑已久的自我，近乎潛意識地爆發出來，口中傾吐出：「自由，自由，自由!」，諷刺的是，就在她開始為自己而活，享受如獲重生的喜悅時，丈夫突然返家，她失落絕望之情，導致心臟病發猝死，醫生當場診斷馬勒夫人是過於高興丈夫生還，以至心臟病發促猝死。

　　凱特蕭邦選擇馬勒夫人的死，而不是她自主意識的復活作結局，意謂凱特蕭邦對當時美國女權鐵板一塊，牢不可破的悲觀，讓這「一小時的故事」也成了馬勒夫人一生僅有的自由生命。

 三、閱讀文選

The Story of An Hour

Kate Chopin

　　Knowing that Mrs. Mallard was *afflicted with a heart trouble*（受心臟病所苦），it was her sister Josephine who told *as gently as possible*（儘可能溫柔婉轉）her the news of her husband's death.

Her husband's friend Richards was there, too, near her. It was he who had received the *intelligence*（資訊）of the railroad *disaster*（災難）and found Brently Mallard's name leading the list of "killed."

She did not hear the story with a *paralyzed inability*（癱軟）as many women have heard the same. She *wept*（哭訴）at once, *with sudden, wild abandonment*（快速絕望）, in her sister's arms. When *the storm of grief*（暴風雨般的悲傷）had *spent itself*（出盡）she went away to her room alone. She would have no one follow her.

There stood a *comfortable armchair*（舒服的扶手椅）, facing the open window. Into this she *sank*（沈坐進去）, *pressed down by a physical exhaustion*（生理疲憊的壓迫）that *haunted*（糾纏）her body and seemed to reach into her soul.

She could see in the open square before her house the tops of trees that were all *aquiver with*（充滿）the new spring life. The delicious breath of rain was in the air. In the street below a *peddler*（小販）was crying his *wares*（貨品）. The *notes*（音符）of a distant song which some one was singing *reached her faintly*（縹緲傳來）, and *countless sparrows*（無數的麻雀）were *twittering*（嘰嘰喳喳）in the *eaves*（屋簷）.

There were *patches*（片片）of blue sky showing here and there through the clouds that had met and *piled one above the other*（雲朵層層疊疊）in the west facing her window.

She sat with her head *thrown back upon the cushion of the chair*（把頭往後靠在椅背上）, quite *motionless*（不動的）, except when a *sob*（嗚咽）came up into her throat and *shook*（顫抖）her, as a child who has cried itself to sleep continues to sob in its dreams.

She was young, with a *fair*（白皙）, calm face, whose *lines*（臉上線條）*bespoke*（說出）*repression*（壓抑）and even a certain strength. But now there was a *dull stare*（目光茫然）in her eyes, whose *gaze*（凝望）was fixed away on one of those patches of blue sky. It was not *a glance of reflection*（匆匆沈思的一瞥）, but rather *indicated*（顯示）a *suspension of intelligent thought*（智能思考的暫停）.

There was something coming to her and she was waiting for it, fearfully. What was it? She did not know; it was *too subtle and elusive to name*（太微妙，難以捉摸而莫名）. But she felt it, *creeping*（不知不覺的爬行）out of the sky, reaching toward her through the sounds, the *scents*（氣味）, the color that filled the air.

Now her *bosom rose and fell tumultuously*（內心起伏巨烈）. She was beginning to recognize this thing that was approaching to *possess*（佔有；附身）her, and she was *striving to*（努力）beat it back with her will—*as powerless as her two white slender hands*（無力如她兩隻纖細、白皙的雙手）would have been. When she *abandoned herself*（放任自己）, a little whispered word *escaped her slightly parted lips*（輕輕脫口而出）. She said it over and over under the breath: "free, free, free!" The *vacant stare*（茫然的目光）and the look of terror were gone from her eyes. They stayed *keen and bright*（機敏，有神）. Her *pulses*（心跳）beat fast, and the blood warmed and relaxed every inch of her body.

She did not stop to ask if it were or were not a *monstrous joy*（巨大的快感）that held her. She knew that she would weep again when she saw his face, kind, tender hands *folded*（雙手在胸膛上放好）in death. But she saw a long procession of years to come that would belong to her absolutely. And she opened and *spread her arms out*（伸出雙臂）to them in welcome.

There would be no one to live for during those coming years; she would live for herself. There would be no men and women believe they have a right to *impose a private will upon*（強加意志於）a fellow creature. *A kind intention or a cruel intention*（不論是善意或惡意）made the act seem *no less a crime*（無異於罪）as she looked upon it.

And yet she had loved him—sometimes. Often she had not. What did it matter! What could love *count for*（價值可比）in the face of this possession of *self-assertion*（面對自我肯定的擁有）which she suddenly recognized as the strongest *impulse of her being*（認出是自我的激情）!

"Free! Body and soul free!" she kept whispering.

Josephine *was kneeling*（跪）before the closed door with her lips to the *keyhole*（鑰匙孔）, *imploring for admission*（要求進門）. "Louise, open the door! I beg; open the door—you will make yourself ill. What are you doing, Louise? For heaven's sake open the door."

"Go away. I am not making myself ill." No; she was drinking in a very *elixir of life*（長生不老藥）through that open window.

Her *fancy was running riot*（狂野的幻想）along those days ahead of her. Spring days , and summer days, and all sorts of days that would be her own. It was only yesterday she had thought with a *shudder*（顫抖）that life might be long.

She arose at length and opened the door to her sister's *importunities*（硬拗；強求）. There was a feverish triumph in her eyes, and she *carried herself*（身體姿勢保持）*unwittingly*（無意識地）like a goddess of Victory. She *clasped her sister's waist*（攬…腰）, and together they descended the stairs. Richards stood waiting for them at the bottom.

Some one was opening the front door with a key. It was Brently Mallard who entered, a little *travel-stained*（風塵僕僕）, carrying his *grip-sack*（手提包）and umbrella. He had *been far from*（遠離）the scene of the accident, and did not even know there had been one. He stood *amazed at*（驚訝於）Josephine's *piercing cry*（嘶叫）; at Richards' quick motion to *screen him from the view of his wife*（當Richards擋住不讓他太太Josephine看到馬勒先生）。

When the doctors came they said she had died of heart disease—*of the joy that kills*（馬勒太太死於過度興奮）。

四、作品延伸作業

就女性主義角度言，凱特蕭邦短篇小說《一小時的故事》結局以馬勒夫人的死，作悲劇的結果，妳有何看法？相較威廉福克納《給愛蜜麗的玫瑰》，有何不同的手法與感受？

19 史考特‧費茲傑羅《一個酗酒案例》──美國「失落的一代」與「經濟大恐慌」之代言人

小說特徵

美國「失落的一代」與「經濟大恐慌」之社會現象

史考特‧費茲傑羅
(F. Scott Fitzgerald, 1896 –1940)

I don't want to repeat my innocence. I want the pleasure of losing it again.

-F. Scott Fitzgerald

與其重複我的純真，我寧可享受一再失去祂的樂趣。

──史考特‧費茲傑羅

一、作者短評

　　費茲傑羅，1896年，出生於美國明尼蘇達州的聖保羅市，由於父親經商失敗，只得投靠岳家，過著寄人籬下的生活。大學就讀於普林斯頓大學，1917年從軍，一次大戰結束後，美國進入空前的經濟繁榮，1920年，二十四歲的費茲傑羅首作《塵世樂園》（This Side of Paradise）出版後，一夕爆紅，緊接《輕佻女子與哲學家》（Flappers and Philosophers）、《爵士時代的故事》（Tales of the Jazz Age），都是描述1920年代美國人在歌舞昇平中，產生所謂「失落的一代」（The lost Generation）的空虛、享樂、矛盾的社會現象與生活思想。而驟得大名的費茲傑羅也娶了名門之女Zelda Sayre為妻，為了維持笙歌宴飲的奢華日子，費滋傑羅開始替《星期六晚郵報》（Saturday Evening Post）撰寫了大量連他自己也痛恨的「低俗」（whoring）短篇小說作品，以賺取高額稿酬，這也是為何後世批評他生活腐化、自暴自棄，以致浪費了自己的才華。好時光總是短暫的，緊接而來的三〇年代經濟大恐慌，費滋傑羅飽受妻子精神狀態不佳，負債累累的經濟窘困，加上他本身長久以來的酗酒問題，1940年12月22日，聖誕節前夕，費茲傑羅心臟病發作，過世於加州好萊塢公寓，年僅四十四歲。

　　費茲傑羅一生由浮華以至幻滅的起伏歷程，完全重疊與倒映了美國一九二〇年代「失落的一代」富裕下的縱慾與虛空以至三〇年代「經濟大恐慌（The Great Panic）」財富破滅的歷程，他的作品也成了編年小說，使他成為這二十個年頭的社會與歷史見證，費茲傑羅最著名的小說為《大亨小傳》（The Great Gatsby），堪稱當時美國社會縮影的經典代表。

二、作品介紹

　　費茲傑羅用小說方式解讀自己的人生與孕育自己人生的那個爵士時代（the Jazz Age）——在這個特殊的二〇年代，費茲傑羅已意識到其實金錢才是美國文化中最重要的符號，也是這個符號導致他作品的成功，同時也是這個符號導致了他一生的失敗，費茲傑羅《一個酗酒案例》根本是他個人經驗的自剖小說，屬於他人生最末端的作品，他藉由一第三人稱的護士對一酗酒病例的個案觀察，表現酗酒者的沉迷及無奈。費茲傑羅本人自大學時期就染上飲酒習慣，之後酗酒問題愈來愈嚴重，他的早逝與過於沉溺酒精關係甚大。文中，敘述一位酗酒的卡通畫家（就是費茲傑羅本人的化身）與看顧他戒酒護士的相處，最後只有自殺求以解脫，這無奈見於這位護士明知道他要自殺，卻也無濟於事的默許，費茲傑羅濃濃傳達了他難去酒癮的痛楚與他對那個時代的失落感。

　　費茲傑羅《一個酗酒案例》正好與美國當時社會喧騰已久的一段獨特禁酒歷史有關。如前所述，美國1920至30的背景年代，社會步調堪稱是雲霄飛車的時代，先是一戰後的經濟過熱，紙醉金迷的生活隨之而來，之後，經濟大恐慌，股市慘跌，又千金散去，不少人以跳樓自殺，結束生命，但有樣東西，在這期間卻是死而復生，就是酒。美國人是以「清教」立國，禁慾、簡約是傳統生活原則，酒老早看成是犯罪、家暴和貧窮的根源，社會改革之進步主義運動人士極欲去之而後快，一戰後，生活的糜爛氛圍，終於在民氣可用之下，禁酒被提升至國家意志的高度，在1919年，美國憲法第十八修正案使美國成為禁酒的國家，但這實在也是美國史上最愚蠢的法案，因為，沒有任何東西能夠改造人性，政府可以用法律宣佈酒類為禁品，但卻不可能從人的心中清除喝酒的欲望，1933年，美國在經濟大恐慌下，羅斯福以憲法第十九條修正案撤銷禁酒令，讓苦悶的人民至少有酒澆愁。費茲傑羅除了表達個人酗酒的無奈，無意間也表達了禁酒好比要人民不要抽煙一樣的天真。

三、閱讀文選

An Alcoholic Case

F. Scott Fitzgerald

"Come on—give me the bottle. I told you I'd *stay awake*（保持清醒）. Come on—leave it with me—I'll *leave half in the bottle.*（留個半瓶）"

"You know what Dr. Carter says, I'm too tired to be *fighting*（爭吵）you all night. . . . All right, drink your fool self to death."

Again they *struggled*（爭奪）.

"Once more you try to get it I'll *throw it down*（砸碎）," she said quickly. "I will—on the *tiles*（磁磚）in the bathroom."

"Then I'll step on the broken glass（踩到碎玻璃）—or you'll step on it."

Suddenly she dropped it like a *torpedo*（魚雷）, *sliding underneath*（滑落）her hand and through the open door to the bathroom.

It was on the floor in pieces and everything was silent for a while. She began to worry that he would have to go into the bathroom and might cut his feet. With a sudden *resurgence of conscience*（良心發現）she got up and put a chair in front of the bathroom door. She had wanted to sleep because he had got her up early that morning and she hadn't been home all day.

She sat down in the *rocker*（搖椅） but she was no longer sleepy; there was plenty to *enter on the chart*（寫報告）and she could make so many:

Tried to get bottle of *gin*（琴酒）. Threw it away and broke it.

She *corrected*（修改）it to read:

In the struggle it dropped and was broken. *Patient*（病人）was generally *difficult*（難搞）.

She added in her report: I never want to go on *an alcoholic case*（戒酒照護案）again.

She was tired and didn't want to clean up the glass on the bathroom floor. But she decided finally to clean up the glass first; *on her knees*（跪下）, searching a last piece of it, she thought: —It was so *utterly senseless*（完全沒道理）—as she put a *bandage*（紗布）on her finger where she had cut it while picking up the glass she made up her mind she would never take an alcoholic case again.

But when she sat down in the chair she looked at his face, white and *exhausted*（疲憊不堪）, and counted his breathing again, wondering why it had all happened. He had been so nice today, drawn her *a whole strip of his cartoon*（一長片的卡通）just for fun and given it to her. She was going to have it *framed*（裱褙）.

It was early the next evening in the hall of Mrs. Hixson's Agency（人力介紹公司）. In a moment Mrs. Hixson came out and, *signaled*（示意）her into the office.

"I got your call from the hotel," she began.

Mrs. Hixson was a very *efficient*（效率的）woman. She had been a nurse and had gone through the worst of it. She *swung*（轉身）around suddenly from the desk.

"Oh, it wasn't bad, Mrs. Hixson. He didn't know what he was doing and he didn't hurt me in any way. I was *thinking much more of my reputation with you*（我考慮信譽對妳公司的影響）. He was really nice all day yesterday."

"But one minute you say you'll never go on an alcoholic case again and the next minute you say you want to go back to one."

"I think I *overestimated*（高估）how difficult it was. Really, I think I could help him."

Getting off the bus, she went down the long steps to the hotel, feeling a little *exalted*（自豪）. She was going to take care of him because nobody else would, and because the best people of her *profession*（專業）had been interested in the cases that nobody else wanted.

She knocked at his study door. He answered it himself. He was in dinner clothes even to a derby hat—but minus his *studs*（袖扣）and tie.

He broke into a *genial, indifferent*（溫和淡然的）smile.

"I thought you had *quit*（放棄）me," he said casually.

"I thought I had, too."

"Who are you going to see?" she asked.

"It's the President's secretary," he said. "I had an *awful time*（苦日子）trying to get ready. I was about to give up when you came in. Will you order me some *sherry*（雪莉酒）?"

"One glass," she agreed *wearily*（厭倦地）…

She went behind him and tied his tie—his shirt was already *thumbed out of press*（被姆指印沾污）where he had put in the studs, and she suggested:

"Won't you *put on*（穿）another one, if you've got to meet some people you like?"

"All right, but I want to do it myself."

"Why can't you let me help you?" she demanded in *exasperation*（憤怒）. "Why can't you let me help you with your clothes? What's a nurse for—what good am I doing?"

He sat down suddenly on the *toilet seat*（馬桶蓋）.

"All right—go on."

"Now don't *grab my wrist*（別抓我的手腕）," she said, and then, "Excuse me."

"Don't worry. It didn't hurt. You'll see in a minute."

"Now watch this," he said. "One—two—three."

She *pulled up the undershirt*（掀起內衫）; *simultaneously*（同時）*he thrust*（刺入）*the crimson—grey point of the cigarette*（火紅的煙頭）like a *dagger*（匕首）against his heart. He said "Ouch!" as a *stray spark fluttered down*（火花濺落）against his stomach.

"You've had a hard time with that, I guess," she said lightly. "Won't it ever *heal*（痊癒）?"

"Never."

"Well, it's no excuse for what you're doing to yourself."

He turned his great brown eyes on her, *aloof, confused*（疏離、茫然）. He signaled to her, in one second, his Will to Die, and for all her training and experience she knew she could never do anything *constructive*（有建設性的）with him. She knew death—she had heard it, smelt it, but she had never seen it before it entered into anyone."

She tried to express it next day to Mrs. Hixson: "It's not like anything you can *beat*（擊敗）—no matter how hard you try. It's just that you can't really help them and it's so discouraging（氣餒）—it's all for nothing."

四、作品延伸作業

海明威《白象似的群山》與史考特・費茲傑羅費茲傑羅《一個酗酒案例》，將美國二〇年代「失落的一代」的情境，像女子墮胎的絕望，男人不想負責任的無所謂及酗酒者放棄一切希望的空虛，一語道盡。何謂美國「失落的一代」，背景與內容為何？

薛吾德・安德森《林中之死》
——生與死的奧秘美學

小說特徵

美國資本文明下的畸形人格

薛吾德・安德森
(Sherwood Anderson,1876 – 1941)

A thing so complete has its own beauty.

-Sherwood Anderson

一件如此完整的事情必有其美麗。

——薛吾德・安德森

一、作者短評

薛吾德安德森（Sherwood Anderson），1876年，生於美國俄亥俄州，由於父親經商失敗，酗酒過世後，從此漂流不定，十四歲年紀的安德森只能到處工作，挑起支撐家庭擔子。

薛吾德安德森之後從軍、念大學，結婚、生子，眼看幸福生活到來時，1912年，安德森精神崩潰，拋家棄子，回到芝加哥，決心進行寫作生涯。1919年，安德森出版《小城畸人》（Winesburg, Ohio），一炮而紅，他在書中羅列著上百個人世間之謂「真理」─有童貞（virginity）與欲望（passion）、節儉（thrift）與放蕩（profligacy）、健康與財富、冷漠（carelessness）與遺棄（abandon）等價值觀。安德森以為正是這些真理使人變成「畸形」，《小城畸人》表達了安德森濃厚的鄉村主義和懷舊情節，流露出安德森反工業文明和資本主義倫理思想，創立了「芝加哥文藝復興」（Chicago literary renaissance, 1912─1925）學派，對美國20世紀重要作家福克納、海明威、史坦貝克等人，皆有重要的影響，是美國文學史上重要的起承人物。但薛吾德安德森從此卻糾纏於婚姻，安德森一生結婚四次的離合之中，作品也大不如前，深受他影響的海明威，就不止一次為安德森感到遺憾。

1941年，薛吾德安德森在巴拿馬過逝，年64。在他埋骨所在的維吉尼亞墓碑上，刻寫「生命，而非死亡，才是偉大的冒險」（"Life, Not Death, is the Great Adventure."）

二、作品分析

　　薛吾德安德森《林中之死》是由第一人稱的敘事者，重述一件蘊積多年，小時候發生的故事，文中所爭的不是那一個才是事情真相的版本，而是自述者所謂的「一件完整的事情，必有其美麗。」，表達作者企圖了解生命與死亡的奧秘，找尋人在每天平凡生活中的美麗與意義。

　　薛吾德安德森擅用人事的畸形，來表現工業社會所造成人內心的創傷，這些作品側重現代生活中的怪誕和病態，安德森特別在對女人描述時，向她們傾注了關注與同情。《林中之死》是敘事者根據他個人的經驗去附會事實，來紀錄他童年時候，對一位老太太的記憶，她一生坎坷，晚景淒涼，自出生作人養女被虐待，到遇人不淑，丈夫、兒子稍有不順，動輒對她打罵，平常，靠著賣雞蛋換取食物，只有鎮上的屠夫願意跟她講話，順帶奉送一些內臟、骨頭作為她的餵狗食物，她一生的過程就是不停地餵食丈夫、兒子與一大群的雞、狗、馬、牛，而毫無怨言。一天，她周而復始的帶著她的狗群，去鎮上用蛋換取食物，並取得屠夫較以往更豐富的奉贈，在返回家中的路上，她改走了林中小徑，在樹下坐下來休息的時候，安靜的過世，她的狗群，有如儀式般圍繞著她奔跑，當獵人發現她屍體時，「看起來是那麼白皙、可愛，有如大理石，狹小的肩軀，在死亡時，宛如少女的美麗身體。」死亡與美麗反畫上了等號。

《林中之死》是安德森暗示回憶是藝術題材滋生的寶庫，記憶中的靜態景象或畫面亦屬藝術表現之泉源，《林中之死》正是以他童年漫不經心的記憶開始，經過長年的想像與老太太遭遇的縈繞心弦，到最後，在透過經驗與想像力認識別人的我，從而找到本身自我的意義，促成了一篇結構完美藝術品的產生，是安德森的美學典型之作。

三、閱讀文選

Death In The Woods

Sherwood Anderson

　　She was an old woman and lived on a farm near the town in which I lived. All small—town people have seen such old women, but no one knows much about them. She may own a few *hens*（母雞）and have eggs to sell. She brings them in a *basket*（籃子）and takes them to a *grocer*（雜貨店主）. There she *trades*（交易）them in. She gets some *salt pork*（醃肉）and some *beans*（大豆）. Then she gets a pound or two of *sugar*（糖）and some *flour*（麵粉）.

　　Afterwards（之後）she goes to the *butcher's*（肉舖）and asks for some dog—meat. The old farm woman got some *liver*（肝）and a soup—bone. She never visited with any one, and as soon as she got what she wanted she *lit out*（匆忙離去）for home. It made quite a *load*（負載）for such an old body. No one *gave her a lift*（拉她一把）and never noticed an old woman like that.

The old woman was nothing special. She was one of the nameless ones that *hardly*（幾乎沒有）any one knows, but she got into my thoughts. Her name was Grimes. She married Jake and had a son and daughter, but the daughter died. Jake always had a lot of big dogs around the house. He was always trading horses when he wasn't stealing something and had a lot of *poor bony ones*（骨瘦如柴的馬）about. Also he kept three or four pigs and a *cow*（母牛）. They were all *pastured*（放牧）in the *few acres*（幾畝地）. People did not trust him. When the son grew up he was just like the father. Although the son was twenty—one, he had already *served a term in jail*（坐過牢）. They *got drunk*（酒醉）together. If there wasn't anything to eat in the house the old man *gave* his old woman *a cut*（像手刀的打法）over the head.

So, to feed *stock*（牲畜）was her job. How was she going to get everything fed?—that was her problem. The pigs had to be fed so they would be grown up and could be *butchered*（宰殺）*in the Fall*（秋天）. The dogs had to be fed. There wasn't enough *hay*（乾草）in the *barn*（穀倉）for the horses and the cow. If she didn't feed the chickens how could they *lay eggs*（生蛋）? Without eggs to sell how could she get things in town, things she had to have to keep the life of the farm going?

One day in Winter the old woman went off to town with a few eggs and the dogs followed her. She did not get started until nearly three o'clock and the snow was heavy. She had an old *grain bag*（穀袋）in which she carried her eggs. She would get a little meat *in exchange for*（交換）the eggs, some salt pork, a little sugar, and some coffee perhaps. It might be the butcher（肉販）would give her a piece of liver.

When she had got to town and was trading in her eggs the dogs lay by the door outside. *She did pretty well*（交易出奇的好）, got the things she needed, *more than she had hoped*（好過預期）. Then she went to the butcher and he gave her some liver and some dog—meat.

The old woman had to get back before darkness came if she could. The dogs followed at her heels, *sniffing at*（嗅到）the heavy grain bag she had *fastened on*（固定）her back. It was hard when she had to *crawl over fences*（爬過圍籬）and once she fell over and landed in the snow. The dogs went *frisking about*（狗群圍繞嬉鬧跳動）. She had to struggle to get to her feet again, but she made it. The point of climbing over the fences was that there was a *short cut*（捷徑）over a hill and through a woods. She was afraid she couldn't make it. And then, besides, the stock had to be fed. There was a little hay left and a little corn. Perhaps her husband and son might come home drunk. It would be well to have something in the house when they came back.

With the *pack*（打包）on her back she went painfully along across an open field, *wading in*（跋涉進入）the deep snow, and got into the woods. Just over the top of the hill, where the woods was *thick*（茂密）, there was a small *clearing*（空地）. There was a *path*（道路）which ran along the side of the clearing, and when she got there the old woman sat down to rest at the foot of a tree.

She must have slept for a time. The dogs in the clearing, before the old woman, had caught two or three rabbits and their immediate hunger had been satisfied. They began to play, running in circles in the clearing. Round and round they ran, each dog's nose at the tail of the next dog. The dogs made no sound. They ran around and around in the circle.

It may have been that the old woman saw them doing that

before she died. She may have awakened once or twice and looked at the strange sight with *dim*（迷濛）old eyes.

She wouldn't be very cold now, just *drowsy*（昏睡）. *Life hangs on a long time*（還維持生命狀態一陣子）. She may have dreamed of her girlhood. Her dreams couldn't have been very pleasant. Not many pleasant things had happened to her. The running of the dogs may have been a kind of death ceremony.

The old woman died softly and quietly. When she was dead and when one of the Grimes dogs had come to her and had found her dead all the dogs stopped running.

They gathered about her.

They *dragged*（拖拉）the old woman's body out into the open clearing. When she was found, a day or two later, the dress had been torn from her body clear to the *hips*（臀部）, but the dogs had not touched her body. Her body was *frozen stiff*（凍僵）when it was found, and the shoulders were so narrow and the body so *slight*（嬌小）that in death it looked like the body of some charming young girl.

Such things happened in towns of the Middle West, on farms near town, when I was a boy. A hunter out after rabbits found the old woman's body and did not touch it. The town marshal was a large man whose leg had been injured in the Civil War. He *limped*（跛行）rapidly along the road. My brother and I followed *at his heels*（跟隨著）, and as we went other men and boys joined the crowd.

It had grown dark by the time we got to where the old woman had left the road but the moon had come out. The marshal was thinking there might have been a murder. He kept asking the hunter questions. The husband and son were found somewhere and brought to town and there was an attempt to connect them with the woman's death, but it did not work. They had perfect enough *alibis*（不在場證明）.

However, the town was against them. They had to get out. Where they went I never heard.

Darkness comes quickly on such Winter nights, but the full moon made everything clear. My brother and I stood near the tree, beneath which the old woman had died.

She did not look old, lying there in that light, frozen and still. One of the men turned her over in the snow and I saw everything. My body *trembled with*（顫抖）some strange *mystical*（神秘的）feeling and so did my brother's. It might have been the cold.

Neither of us had ever seen a woman's body before. It may have been the snow, *clinging to*（黏附）the frozen flesh, that made it look so white and lovely, so like *marble*（大理石）.

The whole thing, the story of the old woman's death, was to me as I grew older like music heard from far off.

The woman who died was one *destined to*（命中注定）feed animal life. Anyway, that is all she ever did. She fed animal life in cows, in chickens, in pigs, in horses, in dogs, in men. Her daughter had died in childhood and with her one son. On the night when she died she was hurrying homeward, bearing on her body food for animal life.

She died in the clearing in the woods and even after her death continued feeding animal life.

A thing so complete has its own beauty.

I shall not try to emphasize the point. I speak of that only that you may understand why I have been *impelled to*（非得）try to tell the simple story over again.

四、作品延伸作業

二十世紀後，資本主義社會已到了堅固的社會分工，其實大部人都已像薛吾德安德森《林中之死》老太太一樣，周而復始奉行一事，直到生命最後一秒。妳喜歡這種「安定」的生活嗎？妳會怎麼改變？

文學視界44　PG1047

小說的密碼
——人性與關懷

編　　著 / 涂成吉
責任編輯 / 廖妘甄
圖文排版 / 詹凱倫
封面設計 / 王嵩賀

發 行 人 / 宋政坤
法律顧問 / 毛國樑　律師
出版發行 / 秀威資訊科技股份有限公司
　　　　　114台北市內湖區瑞光路76巷65號1樓
　　　　　電話：+886-2-2796-3638　傳真：+886-2-2796-1377
　　　　　http://www.showwe.com.tw
劃撥帳號 / 19563868　戶名：秀威資訊科技股份有限公司
　　　　　讀者服務信箱：service@showwe.com.tw
展售門市 / 國家書店（松江門市）
　　　　　104台北市中山區松江路209號1樓
　　　　　電話：+886-2-2518-0207　傳真：+886-2-2518-0778
網路訂購 / 秀威網路書店：http://www.bodbooks.com.tw
　　　　　國家網路書店：http://www.govbooks.com.tw

2013年9月　BOD一版
定價：230元

國家圖書館出版品預行編目

小說的密碼：人性與關懷 / 涂成吉編著. -- 一版. -- 臺北
市：秀威資訊科技, 2013. 09
　　面；　　公分. -- (文學視界 ; PG1047)
BOD版
ISBN 978-986-326-183-4 (平裝)

1. 短篇小說　2. 文學評論

812.78　　　　　　　　　　　　　　　102016585

讀者回函卡

感謝您購買本書，為提升服務品質，請填妥以下資料，將讀者回函卡直接寄回或傳真本公司，收到您的寶貴意見後，我們會收藏記錄及檢討，謝謝！如您需要了解本公司最新出版書目、購書優惠或企劃活動，歡迎您上網查詢或下載相關資料：http:// www.showwe.com.tw

您購買的書名：_____

出生日期：_____年_____月_____日

學歷：□高中 (含) 以下　　□大專　　□研究所 (含) 以上

職業：□製造業　□金融業　□資訊業　□軍警　□傳播業　□自由業
　　　□服務業　□公務員　□教職　　□學生　□家管　　□其它_____

購書地點：□網路書店　□實體書店　□書展　□郵購　□贈閱　□其他

您從何得知本書的消息？

　　□網路書店　□實體書店　□網路搜尋　□電子報　□書訊　□雜誌
　　□傳播媒體　□親友推薦　□網站推薦　□部落格　□其他_____

您對本書的評價：(請填代號　1.非常滿意　2.滿意　3.尚可　4.再改進)

　　封面設計____　版面編排____　內容____　文／譯筆____　價格____

讀完書後您覺得：

　　□很有收穫　□有收穫　□收穫不多　□沒收穫

對我們的建議：_____

_____

_____

_____

11466
台北市內湖區瑞光路 76 巷 65 號 1 樓

秀威資訊科技股份有限公司　　　收

BOD 數位出版事業部

....

（請沿線對折寄回，謝謝！）

姓　　名：＿＿＿＿＿＿＿＿　年齡：＿＿＿＿　性別：□女　□男

郵遞區號：□□□□□

地　　址：＿＿＿＿＿＿＿＿＿＿＿＿＿＿＿＿＿＿＿＿

聯絡電話：(日)＿＿＿＿＿＿＿＿　(夜)＿＿＿＿＿＿＿＿＿

E - m a i l：＿＿＿＿＿＿＿＿＿＿＿＿＿＿＿＿＿＿＿＿＿